EGG AND BACON

By

Lindale Thompson

1

EGG AND BACON

Cover art by Natasa Thompson

This book is dedicated to Miriam Elizabeth Parker,
my grandmother.

"Mama, it's a source of great comfort to know that
you are watching over me"

Contents

Prologue

Andrew Smalls took a long, deep breath. The last three years felt like a relentless, brutal battle for survival that had left him physically and mentally exhausted. Anxiety gripped him like a vice. He couldn't sleep, he couldn't eat, and the tension in the pit of his stomach left him constantly on the verge of throwing up. At the age of twenty-seven, he was already losing his hair.

It was a sunny Friday afternoon. He was standing in front of Tottenham Court Road train station, the permanent worry lines on his black face making him seem older than his years. His hair, although a short crop, was badly in need of a cut. His white shirt was open at the top and his tie was hanging loosely around his neck; sweat stains were visible under his armpits. His trousers were black, as were his slightly worn shoes. A small backpack was strapped to his back.

Andrew took another deep breath, slowly, slowly, trying to count to ten; he had to try to remain calm. Andrew tried closing his eyes and to picture a calm, serene scene—a tropical beach, a beautiful sunset, or even the English countryside—but the multiple sounds of the city got in the way. He found it difficult to cut out the sound of the traffic, the blaring sirens, the people walking and talking, and even the rustling of shopping bags. They all proved to be a distraction. Andrew's body shook with nervous tension. The battle he had fought earlier that day played on his mind, and the little energy he had left was now being drained by the frustration and anger he felt.

Andrew watched as a group of ladies briskly walked past. He guessed that they were probably secretaries. There was always the distinct possibility that they weren't, but Andrew doubted that, as they had what he considered 'the secretary look': tottering heels, suits and lots of makeup. Several of them had that strange way of holding a handbag, where it dangled down by the handle. He wondered if they were aware of how bland, robotic and uninspiring they looked. They probably worked in some boring corporate office, where they typed endless letters and gossiped around coffee machines, happy to be travelling like caged animals every day just so they could proudly boast about the fact that they were earning a living. He heard one of them mention that their boss was going to kill them for coming back late from lunch for the third time. Andrew wondered, in the grand scheme of things, was that as important as his own daily battle for survival? It was a battle that saw him not only trying to make a living, but somehow trying to hold on to his sanity as well. Life felt like this endless struggle that repeated the same thing over and over again, with little prospect of anything ever changing. Taking off his tie, Andrew entered the train station, his eyes filled with tears.

PART ONE

The Kaff

The café stood out like a sore thumb, sandwiched between the more upmarket eateries that dotted along the famous Portobello Road. Among the various speciality coffee shops of the world, it stubbornly stood out as a member of a dying breed—the greasy spoon café. The set up was very basic other than a modern coffee machine and there were no airs and graces as far as the menu was concerned. Several variations of the traditional full English formed the basis of its breakfast menu, all served up on cheap china. The furniture was a throwback to decades before, with its mustard-coloured Formica tables and plastic chairs. The walls were covered with faded floral wallpaper, as well as two prints of Notting Hill from the 19th century. Two pictures— one of the Queen and the other of the English Flag— hung side by side at the front of the counter. There was also a large flat-screen television hanging from the ceiling. On a small table next to the counter, there was a tray for customers to collect their knives and forks. The Cafe was simply known as *"The Café"* or, in the vernacular of its regular customers; *"The Kaff."*

The exterior of the café featured large windows that were covered with paper plates advertising a number of dishes and special offers.

During the week, the majority of The Café's customers were poor, working-class mothers. They would arrive throughout the morning, order breakfast, and then collect chairs and tables and place them strategically outside. By nine o'clock, the exterior of the café would be filled with large pushchairs, barking dogs and screaming children; the fumes from cigarette smoke forming a subconscious wall that guarded against the onslaught of property developers, overpriced coffee shops, yummy mummies and anything else that intruded on their rapidly-fading way of life. For these customers, the social apartheid that represented present-day life in Notting Hill was a reality and anyone that didn't belong to it, received a sneer as they walked past.

On Saturdays, the market traders would join the regulars and use the café as a base of operations. Here they would eat, use the toilet, and generally moan about the state of business on Portobello Road. The incompetent council, sky-high rents and the general erosion of the sense of community were frequent topics discussed. One of the more well-known market traders often appeared as an extra on any film that used Notting Hill as a backdrop. His larger-than-life personality, bodybuilder physique, and long blond hair ensured that he was in demand for any scenes requiring an authentic trader from the area. He could often be found holding a handful of headshot pictures, offering a signed autograph copy for just a pound. He also enjoyed telling stories of his brushes with the stars, including his one-night-stand with an English actress who went on to make it big in the states.

The occasional tourist would pop in for a meal, eager to sample what they considered to be typical English food. It did not escape their notice that the food was also the cheapest on the market, allowing limited budgets to stretch a little longer.

On Sundays, different groups would pass through the café's doors. Firstly, there were the boisterous party types, whose remedy for curing massive hangovers from the night before was to stuff themselves with a traditional full English breakfast. They were then joined by the local football team, who piled in, ate breakfast, and optimistically left the café with the sincere intention of beating their opponents, even though they hadn't won a game in years. At around 11:30 a.m., the football fans would start to arrive, making sure that they had enough time to order food and drinks as well as reserve their seats in anticipation of spending a day watching Sunday football. Over the years, many of the local pubs had undergone major refurbishments to attract a more prosperous clientele. These men, used to frequenting the pubs to watch the games, now found the pretentious atmosphere of these upgraded venues not to their liking and would move to a "proper pub" each time. However, as more and more pubs joined in the trend of refurbishment, they now found themselves being marginalised. Seeing a gap in the market, Alfie (the café owner) bought a large flat-screen TV, an extended liquor licence, and advertised heavily. Soon, the café became the place to be if you wanted to watch the games with something resembling the big match atmosphere.

Alfie was a bald, large, overweight Egyptian man who walked around with a permanent smile. Alfie's real name was Foud but he had decided to give himself the same name as the character in *EastEnders*. It was a proper English name to which his customers would be able to relate, and this, along with an exaggerated cockney accent, were the tools he utilised to increase trade.

Alfie always came to work in a three-piece suit, no matter the weather. He had two of them and would wear them on alternate days, accompanied by a large gold chain around his neck and several rings on his fingers. Alfie felt it was important to always look the part of a successful businessman. He was convinced that having a successful business combined with his unique sense of style meant that he was an attractive proposition to women. However, he felt he had to be careful not to get too involved with any woman or even worse, get married; marriage was an institution that was designed to eat into a successful man's profit margins. He felt women instantly sensed that this was his perception—after all, what other possible reason could there be for women not falling at his feet?

Alfie loved to create a family atmosphere in the café. He recognised that a lot of his customers found it hard to make ends meet and as such, it was a common occurrence for him to allow them to have a free breakfast on the promise that as soon as their benefit cheque arrived, they would repay him. For the most part, his customers would repay him or, if they couldn't afford the cash, they would give him a present of some kind. Alfie's home was filled with presents of all types: knitted jumpers (a popular choice), alcohol, and even homemade cakes. Many of his customers even went as far as working a shift for him. Thankfully, dishwashing proved to be a popular job among his customers, as although Alfie had a dishwashing machine, he never enjoyed doing that job. Stuffing dirty dishes into a machine was not what a successful businessman should be doing!

Alfie loved entering his café in the morning. It was the culmination of years of hard work that had seen him come to England as a young lad, where he had worked endless hours in low-paid catering jobs and taken NVQ courses until he could scrape together the money to have his own business. He loved making a show of putting on his apron at the start of the day, turning on the machines, and enjoying the look of the empty café, knowing that for many of his customers, this was a major part of their lives. Alfie loved to cook—it was the job he loved doing the most. Alfie also served all the fancy coffees and herbal teas, since his only full-time member of staff, Gladys, refused to serve anything fancier than basic filter coffee and traditional builder's tea. As far as Gladys was concerned, serving anything other than this was yet another example of foreigners influencing the British way of life, and she had no intention of encouraging that.

Gladys wore a permanent scowl as if it was a badge of honour. She often claimed to be seventy; however, everyone suspected that she was at least eighty-five. She was a large, overweight woman with grey uncombed hair that was peppered with bald patches. Although she had dentures, nine times out of ten she would forget to put them in for work. Other times she would take them out, put them in a glass of fizzy water and place them on the counter, reasoning that it was a good way of keeping them clean. She wore a grey shapeless dress that despite her large size, was still too big for her. Gladys smoked so much that she actually lost her voice; when she spoke, she made a rasping sound. The stench of her cigarette smoke was something that always hit you several seconds before she arrived at your table.

Gladys treated the customers with a large dose of contempt for daring to interrupt her numerous cigarette breaks. They had a lot of nerve expecting her to take orders, take meals to their tables, and clean up after them as if she was a slave. Customers took it upon themselves to clear their own tables rather than endure her swearing at them for behaving as if the café was some sort of a hotel and putting Alfie and her "In the shit!"

Gladys suffered numerous health problems. There were times when she would be off for weeks on end, only to suddenly appear for work again whenever Alfie suggested it was perhaps now time for her to retire.

Alfie realised that although business was fairly reasonable, he would have a lot more customers coming through the doors if he got rid of Gladys. He kept her on because he lacked the courage to fire her and it was, in his mind, the right thing to do. Besides, at her age and state of health, Alfie reasoned that she didn't have long to live, so he could afford to wait. Above all else, Alfie was a patient man.

Friday, 1:15 p.m.

Andrew Smalls sat in the café. In front of him was a cup of coffee and a half-eaten sandwich, as well as a cheap notebook. It was roughly an hour since he had stood at Tottenham Court Road train station. Andrew liked to sit facing the window of the café, so he could watch what was going on outside. Gladys was outside, smoking a cigarette and glaring at the passers-by. The warm weather seemed to lift people's spirits; there were lots of smiles and fewer clothes on display. People were walking in that annoyingly slow way that they do when they want to bask in the rays of the sun. Andrew never related to the sudden outlet of joy people seemed to get whenever the sun came out. Why should the weather have this effect on people? If your life was miserable in the first place, why should the sun change that?

Besides Andrew, there were three other people in the café. Slouching against the counter and talking to Alfie was a tall, light-skinned Jamaican man in his seventies. He was remarkably good-looking for his age and his hair was short with a side parting. Sitting on one of the tables was a man who was roughly in his early fifties. He had uncombed hair and was wearing a badly creased suit. Sitting nearby on another table was a homeless lady with long, uncombed hair. She was surrounded by four overflowing shopping bags and was reading a copy of *The Stage* newspaper. The other tables, although empty, were filled with dirty plates from previous customers.

Andrew stared at the prints of Notting Hill; one of them was a print of Notting Hill tube station.

However, he couldn't see anything that indicated that it was a tube station. He could make out the buildings that used to stand there; he assumed they were on the site of the modern-day banks. In front of one of the buildings was a horse and carriage. He thought it was a bit much to expect to see the familiar tube station sign, but surely there should have been some sort of a sign for it? He found himself drawn to the picture, mainly because he was curious to know what life had been like in Notting Hill during the 19th century, and what those people would have made of Notting Hill if they had been alive today. For a split second, he was tempted to try and sketch parts of the picture, but quickly abandoned the thought.

Andrew allowed the sound of laughter to distract him and his attention was drawn to the counter, where the discussion between the Jamaican man and Alfie was becoming animated. The Jamaican man's outfit was certainly colourful. He wore a purple shirt that was open to the waist so that it displayed an impressive amount of chest hair. This was accompanied by a pair of yellow trousers and white shoes. Next to the man was a guitar case that was covered with stickers of all shapes and sizes.

"Cliff, it can't have been that bad," said Alfie.

"That bad?" exclaimed Cliff. "It was a lot worse. We were invited to this country, so we expected to be welcomed with open arms. There was no way we expected to be treated the way we were. Have you ever heard the saying, *"No Blacks, no Irish, no Dogs"*? That's what we had to face whenever we went looking for a job or a place to live."

"No way," replied Alfie.

"Yeah man," replied Cliff.

17

At that point, the man sitting at the table suddenly got up and started to pace up and down the café. Alfie and Cliff silently watched him. Andrew caught the bemused expression on Cliff's face.

"Hey Bea!" exclaimed Cliff, looking at the homeless lady. "How's things?"

"Good," replied Bea, peering away from her newspaper, a pair of thick glasses perched on her nose. "I've got an audition next week; I need to prepare for it. It would be a lot easier, if not for all this racket."

Bea pointedly glared at the man.

There was an eerie silence as everyone became engrossed in watching the man as he paced up and down the café, mumbling to himself. Andrew noticed that there was a black cloth napkin neatly laid out on the table, along with a tall half-filled glass of red wine and the bottle that went with it. The man walked up to the table, took a sip of wine, then grabbing a packet of cigarettes out of his coat pocket, he walked outside the café for a smoke.

Cliff shook his head.

"The professor is at it again," he mumbled.

"Gets on my fucking nerves!" shouted Bea.

Andrew was amused at the fact that Cliff called the man "The Professor". He certainly reminded him of a few of the lecturers he'd had at university— social misfits who, for all their intelligence, would find it a struggle to live in the normal world with a job and a wife. The world of academia was a safe place for them to hide.

"Well, like I was saying," butted in Cliff, changing the subject, "England was a rough place to live in those days."

"I heard all about those riots they use to have, back in the day. Did you ever see any of that?" asked Alfie.

"See them, see them!" exclaimed Cliff. "I was in them, mate. I've given many a racist white man a good hiding in my time. It was so heart-breaking to see how living in England affected many of us. We had to deal with the stress of trying to make our way, being away from our families, and the bloody cold weather. I knew some guys that were so depressed, they ended up committing suicide. I must admit, the racism hardened me. I didn't handle it very well and back then; I was a real angry young man who was not afraid to let my fists do the talking."

Andrew took note of Cliff's physique; he was still in excellent shape and it wasn't too hard to imagine him being a real tough guy in his younger days.

Cliff continued: "Back in the day, I used to hang out with some real hard men; ex-servicemen who fought alongside the British for Queen and Country, who had seen things that no one should ever experience in their lifetime. They were proper hard men that didn't stand for any racist nonsense. You messed with one of us and you'd know about it. I lost count of the amount of ass-whipping we dished out. The police, the local gangsters … everyone knew enough about us to just let us go about our business. And let me tell you—we did!"

"I was tough, but I wasn't the toughest by any means. However, I did have the biggest chip on my shoulder; I always had a point to prove. I used to dress up in my best suit, borrow a white sheep-skin coat from a mate of mine, and then make sure I had a knife in my back pocket. In them days, we didn't use guns, it was either fists or knives. Then I would hit the town, making sure that I was stepping out with not just one white girl, but two. I would find the bar where the toughest, roughest white racists would hang out and make my entrance." Cliff laughed out loud at the memory. "Let me tell you, if looks could kill... But the bastards didn't dare touch me because if they did, a couple of them would go down that night. And even if they did get to harm me, they knew that they would have to deal with my friends, and that would not be pretty. Yeah man, those were the days. The ones with a bit more courage would walk up to me and ask if they could buy the girls a drink. Man, I would take my alligator-skinned wallet out of my pocket and take out a few fifty-pound notes, then I'd slap them on the bar and tell them, "I can stand this!""

Cliff roared with laughter, and Andrew found himself smiling. He imagined this was a story Cliff had told many times before.

A pretty oriental lady suddenly burst into the café. She was in her early forties, with long silver hair which covered her back. She was dressed from head to toe in expensive designer gear; her mini-skirt and simple blouse designed to emphasis an amazing figure that had been honed by many hours spent in the gym. She wore tall boots and bracelets right up to her elbows. Despite her expensive clothing, she possessed the raw stench of someone that had suffered a lifetime of abusive relationships. She looked around the café and then confidently strode up to the counter.

"Hey Pearl, how's life?" asked Cliff

"Okay, very busy, customers running me ragged," replied Pearl. "Alfie, get me a white coffee, extra milky."

"You know that offer still stands? Why don't you give me a freebie, at least you'll know what a real man feels like," said Cliff

"What? The last time I did that, that toothpick you call a penis barely touched the insides. You would have to pay me to even look at that museum piece again," quipped Pearl as Alfie laughed.

"You're so wrong," laughed Cliff, catching the eye of Andrew, who could barely contain his amusement.

Alfie handed Pearl her coffee. Upon receiving it, she took some sugar from the stand, walked to a table, took the dirty dishes back to the counter, and then sat down, looking at her watch.

Friday, 2:30 p.m.

Andrew took a sip of his coffee, which by now was cold. He winced.

Cliff was leaning on the counter, talking to Alfie. By now, the professor was sitting back at his table, reading a paper. Bea was still studiously reading *The Stage*, which incidentally was upside down. Gladys was outside again, smoking a cigarette. Pearl sat at her table; her coffee long finished. A slim man in his early thirties entered the café; he had mouse-coloured hair and thick, gold-rimmed glasses. He was dressed in a very expensive suit and carried a very large briefcase. He tip-toed towards Pearl, sweat pouring from a very red face; she smiled and mentioned his name. His hands shook as he opened his wallet. He was about to give her cash, when she gestured to him.

"Don't be stupid, not here. Let's go!"

"Of course," he replied. Nervously, he put his wallet back into his pockets.

She escorted him out the door and at the last minute, squeezed his bum, causing the man to jump up nervously. She then turned and winked at Alfie and Cliff, who were watching the encounter and laughing.

Andrew took another sip of cold coffee. The TV was playing music by one of those boy bands that Andrew didn't know and had no desire to know either.

It was the Friday before the Easter bank holiday weekend and Andrew was grateful that his manager had sent him home early once his work was finished.

Being a temp, Andrew was used to working for managers that would give him other tasks to do, just to fill out the time. He'd often overhear managers saying they were going to have to get "their money's worth" while he was forced to stack pencils or staple meaningless documents together, just because he had the nerve to finish his work early.

Although Andrew thought that for the most part, his manager was an okay guy, his constant moaning about his lack of a bonus got on his nerves. As far as Andrew was concerned, this was a guy who had a job that paid somewhere in the region of £40,000 a year. He also didn't seem to have any obvious skills that Andrew was aware of, he simply knew the right people. He certainly had nothing to moan about. He still had his Easter holiday in the Caribbean to look forward to; he would supposedly use that time to "Plan his next move". All Andrew had to look forward to was a bank holiday weekend stuck in the house with barely enough money to buy food, and the prospect of a mind-numbing job to return to on the following Tuesday.

Andrew had spent the best part of the morning trying to recover the thirty pounds that he was owed. He had worked a one-off event as a waiter the week before, filled out his timesheet, and handed it to the banqueting manager. It now appeared that the banqueting manager had misplaced it and because the agency didn't receive it, he wasn't paid. The agency wanted Andrew to take another timesheet back to the hotel and get it re-signed so that he could get paid the following week.

Andrew lost his temper—it wasn't his fault that the timesheet had been lost. Everyone knew he was there; why couldn't the agency or the hotel just pay him now and sort out the paperwork later? Why should he have to suffer because of someone else's mistake? In the end, the agency decided to email a timesheet to the banqueting manager, saying that providing he sent the details back by the Tuesday morning, Andrew would be paid the following Friday. Andrew didn't think it was good enough, but there was nothing else he could do. He was so furious, that he could hardly concentrate on his work. He needed that money.

At least his manager, amid his endless whining, sensed that there was something more to Andrew's frequent toilet breaks other than just loose bowels, and wisely told him to call it a day.

Andrew quickly left the office and, not feeling the urge to go home right away, had headed to the café. By rights, he couldn't even afford the meal. However, he had to try and work out what he needed to do and he felt it would be easier for him to concentrate at the café.

After scrambling to pay his rent, Andrew was down to his last five pounds in the bank, some money on his Oyster Card for travel, and some loose change in his pocket. Andrew looked at his notebook: on the left-hand side, there was a list of all his bills and on the other side, at the top, was the figure £192. This was the amount, prior to taxes, which he expected to be paid the following week.

Andrew sighed. His council tax bill was due next week and with it already in collections, Andrew knew that he would have no choice but to pay it. He had already negotiated a lower bill and didn't think the company would allow him to decrease it any further. His electric bill was also going to come up soon, so he had to think of what he was going to do.

With only one day's work booked for the following week, Andrew fought to overcome the familiar feeling of despair.

Andrew once again considered signing on. The thought of doing that was embarrassing but he had to face the facts that he was in trouble. If he signed on, at the very least, social services could cover his rent. That way he might be able to make some headway with his finances. However, there were significant drawbacks, the chief of which being that he considered the jobcentre staff to be uneducated and unhelpful.

He had once signed on out of desperation, but the sign-on days always seemed to coincide with the days when he finally managed to get work. He found himself having to decide between either signing on or turning down work. After two months of turning down work just so that he could get to the jobcentre, Andrew decided he would rather take his chances looking for work. Also, this meant he could avoid having to endure being treated like a sub-human by mindless morons. These psychopaths had nothing else going for them other than the fact that some deranged person thought it would be fun to place them in a position where they could inflict the most damage on normal people, whose only crime was to want to live a decent life. However, now he realised that he may well have to swallow his pride and look at signing on again. As a realistic option, he simply could not afford to dismiss it.

On the following page of his notebook, Andrew made a list of agencies; some of whom he had worked for, and others he was considering signing up to. As far as he was concerned, his only recourse was to make as many phone calls as possible to get work. Although the following Monday was a bank holiday, he had to use that day to make those calls. There might be a few companies open for business, even on a bank holiday, and he had to try on the off-chance that he could somehow drum up some work. As for the rest of the weekend—he was too skint to do anything else, so the only option he had was to thoroughly clean his flat.

Satisfied with his plan, Andrew leaned back on his chair. He was just about to tuck into his sandwich when the strong scent of cigarette smoke engulfed him and suddenly Gladys appeared, swiftly grabbing the plate off the table.

"You've hardly touched the bloody thing! Honestly, I don't know why we bother!"

Without a backward glance, Gladys dumped the sandwich into the bin.

Saturday, 7:30 a.m.

"The West Indian team is going from bad to worse. We are a shambles, a total shambles!"

The elderly Jamaican man looked around the laundrette as if challenging anyone to respond to his outburst. However, the other customers wisely averted their eyes away from him. Andrew concentrated on putting his clothes into the washing machine. Besides Andrew and the Jamaican man, who sat, legs apart, sporting a flat cap that covered his bald head, there were three other people in the laundrette. The laundry worker was a petite Irish lady who busied herself arranging her service washes. There was also a Spanish man in his late fifties, who stood watching his clothes turning around in the dryer as if it was a television screen, and an African man in his late twenties, who was reading a bible and had two mobile phones on the bench next to him.

The Jamaican man continued his rant. "Line and length, that's how you bowl; line and length, line and length, man!" Raising his voice to a shout, "The West Indian team is a bloody disgrace!"

Suddenly interested, Andrew looked up from his machine.

"Oh, you play?"

"No!" snapped the man, looking at Andrew as if he had just sworn at him. "I can't play!"

Andrew shook his head.

"Don't give me that look, young man. Tend to your clothes; this is big man talk now."

Andrew knew there was no point in talking. Instead, he simply shrugged and closed the door of

27

the washing machine. Andrew couldn't understand why the man was getting excited anyway. As far as Andrew was concerned, cricket was such an incredibly boring sport; only slightly more interesting than watching paint dry.

The Spanish man took some of his clothes out of the dryer and put another coin in to start it up again. He then started to meticulously fold his underwear. Andrew watched him, concluding there must be something mentally wrong with him. After all, who wastes time folding underwear?

It was Saturday and as part of his routine, Andrew would take his clothes to the laundrette as soon as it opened, which was around 7:30 in the morning. The weather was unusually warm for this time of the year, so Andrew could wash some of his clothes and then dry them at home. Like everything nowadays, the price of washing clothes was extremely expensive. Once Andrew had put the money in and the machine had started to wash, he prepared to leave the laundrette.

The African man looked up from his Bible.

"How are you today?"

Andrew sighed, knowing what was coming.

"I'm fine."

"And work? How is that going on?

"Okay."

"That's very good. God bless. I wanted you to know that after our last discussion, I have been praying for you and my invitation to our church still stands."

Andrew remembered the last discussion very clearly; it was a chat that had escalated into a full-scale argument. The African had annoyed him by claiming that Africans were far more successful than

West Indians, as they put a higher emphasis on education and were more adaptable. Andrew had responded by saying that if he believed that, then he had never really studied the history of blacks in Britain, especially the impact of Caribbeans on the British way of life, and that if he wanted to engage in any debate, he should have at least got his facts right. It would have been okay, had the discussion ended there. However, the African man insisted on pressing his point, egged on by the laundry attendant. In the end, he had found himself screaming at the man. Andrew didn't consider himself a violent person, but even he was mystified as to how come he hadn't hit him.

Arguments were a normal activity in the laundrette. Despite coming from varied backgrounds, the people that gathered in the laundrette had one thing in common: they all faced individual challenges whilst living in London. The laundrette was simply a platform to express their frustrations with the world. The laundry attendant, out of sheer boredom, was great at provoking heated discussions. She would spread a tabloid on top of one of the machines and read the news aloud, hoping that someone would take the bait and get annoyed. If there had been a major argument the previous week, she would gently speak to the people involved, asking if they were still upset. Depending on the response she received, she would remind them of the contentious points brought up previously and double-check that they were really okay.

Andrew's guard was already up; his week hadn't ended well, so he wasn't in the most tolerant of moods.

"And my decision not to go anywhere near that church of yours still stands," replied Andrew.

"But my brother, I want to show you a different way to live your life."

"I am not your brother!"

"We are all brothers in the eyes of Christ!"

The laundry attendant looked on.

"What?" exclaimed Andrew, confused.

"I think he means we are all human; we are all one, know what I mean?" chipped in the laundry attendant, her strong Irish accent becoming even more pronounced in her excitement.

"Church is a good thing," added the Jamaican man.

Andrew started to shake in anger.

The laundry attendant, seeing this, started to salivate.

"See, my Caribbean brethren is right, you've simply got to have faith in Jesus," put in the African.

"Faith?" screamed Andrew.

"Yes, faith," repeated the laundry attendant, looking as if she was about to have an orgasm at any minute.

"Why, so I can walk around with that same fucking docile look on my face, just like you?"

"Come on, my brother, don't be like that."

"He's right, that's not nice," the laundry attendant butted in again. For a brief second, Andrew wondered if she was going to pass out.

"You know what, I'm not falling for this," said Andrew. He headed towards the door, only to be physically blocked by the laundry attendant.

"Are you alright, lad?" she asked, showing mock concern.

"He just needs God in his life; we should all pray for him," spoke the African man, clasping his hands together.

Andrew had really had enough.

"Pray for me? You shouldn't be praying for me at all, mate!" exclaimed Andrew. "You should be praying I don't slap you down."

"Come on now, you..." replied the African man.

Andrew interrupted him.

"What the hell happened to you lot! What happened?" Explain that to me?" exclaimed Andrew, in full flow.

"What do you mean, Brother?" replied the African man, with a condescending patience that annoyed Andrew even more.

"Exactly what I said, what the hell happened?"

"I don't understand, what should I explain?"

The African man looked slightly confused, the veneer of patience slowly breaking. The Spanish man took out a dirty handkerchief from his pocket and gave it to the laundry attendant, who by now was sweating profusely.

Andrew started, "At least we could say that we were descended from slaves and our culture was ripped away from us, so we didn't know any better. But you're a proper African, from the motherland. Shouldn't you have your own religion or something? Why are you prancing around, worshipping a white Jesus? I'd have a lot more respect for you if you had some obscure religion I had never heard of, or if you were some sort of a black nationalist. Instead, you walk around with your nose in that Bible, wearing that cheap-looking bargain basement suit, annoying the hell out of people."

"Cheap-looking suit. Hah, hah!" laughed the laundry attendant, looking at the African. "That was funny, you know."

Flustered, the African man moved closer to Andrew.

"Get out my face, you bloody idiot!"

With that, Andrew stormed out of the laundrette.

Saturday, 8:15 a.m.

Andrew was ashamed of himself. He should have known better. He should never have allowed that idiot to get under his skin like that. They had argued about religion before, as Andrew couldn't understand the African man's dogmatic certainty that God existed and that the belief systems of other cultures were incorrect. If he had been a bit more tolerant of other's beliefs, Andrew would have been more supportive. However, as far as he knew, this guy wasn't interested in having a discussion, he just wanted to hear the sound of his own voice, just like the Jamaican man. Andrew was only adding fuel to the fire by indulging him.

Andrew welcomed the slight breeze that brushed against his face; he still couldn't believe how warm it was for this time of the year. He wondered if he should take a walk before going to the flat, if only to clear his head. Portobello market would be busy, with the bulk of the stalls already set up. Local shoppers would be buzzing about, getting their shopping done early in the hope of avoiding the mass arrival of tourists to come. He loved walking around the market, watching the market traders getting ready for the day. In the time that Andrew had lived in the area, he had gotten to know many of the market traders and chatting to them was his way of forgetting his troubles.

He also considered getting a coffee at the café, but quickly dismissed that idea, remembering how Gladys had thrown his food away the day before. Alfie had spotted Andrew's look of shock at the time and had made a promise that he would "look after him". However, after the encounter in the laundrette, having to deal with that nicotine-smelling harpy didn't seem like the smartest way to lift his spirits. Besides, he should be trying to save what little money he had. Andrew had to remind himself that if there was to be any hope for him at all, he had to demonstrate the self-discipline to do what he needed to do. And right now, his priority was to clean the flat.

Andrew lived in the basement flat of a house that had been converted into four flats. There were two other tenants besides Andrew, with the final flat reserved for the landlord, who would pop in occasionally to take care of basic repairs. In common with a lot of houses turned flats in the area, the basement flat had a separate entrance.

As Andrew reached the front of his flat, the door opened from the entrance above him. An overweight lady in her mid-twenties appeared. Her hair was brown with red and blue streaks down the middle, and she carried a cigarette which she puffed on constantly. She was wearing a tight halter top which had a generous amount of breast struggling to pop out. She also wore a pair of those shorts that have frills at the end; the ones that look as if you just left the house and forgot to put on a dress. Seeing a lady wearing those shorts, Andrew wished he had been the one to come up with the idea of women wearing their knickers as outdoor wear. He would have been better off financially as a result, and persuading women that this was a cool look was a stroke of genius in its audacity and its simplicity. Her idiotic fashion sense was completed with tattoos that covered her large thighs, and impossibly high heels that caused her to struggle to stand.

Following her out of the flat were three children, known around the neighbourhood as *The Benetton Kids*. The oldest child was a mixed-race girl (half white, half black), the eldest boy had a distinct Latin or North African look about him, and the youngest boy was white. Following the children was a large, muscular black man, who looked like he could have been a bouncer in a west end club. He wore a white vest, black jeans and trainers. His bald head would have seemed menacing, if not for his wide beaming smile. Andrew figured out that he must be her latest boyfriend. She seemed to change boyfriends the way other people changed socks.

"Alright, Andrew?"

"I'm cool. How's things with you, Shannon?" replied Andrew, making a point to acknowledge the man standing next to her.

"I'm good. Say hello to Andrew, kids."

The two boys meekly muttered "Hello", whereas the girl eyed Andrew suspiciously.

"Where are your manners, Lauren?" shouted Shannon. In one swift movement, Shannon slapped Lauren on the back of her head, which caused her to let out a small squeal of pain before she meekly uttered "Hello". She then started to cry.

"Honestly, no fucking backbone or manners!" muttered Shannon.

Andrew suppressed a wave of sympathy. Having a mother like Shannon must be a nightmare. For Shannon, children were an unhappy inconvenience that interrupted her lifestyle of parties, long boozy sessions and holidays paid for by whomever she happened to be with at the time. Shannon had never held a job for longer than a week, claiming that it was too stressful. She had briefly worked as a cleaner but had stopped because the job was playing havoc with her nails. She didn't like working as a cashier in Tesco, as there were too many customers getting on her nerves. A job as a school dinner lady was definitely off-limits; she hated kids. She had only ever worked at all because the benefits office had threatened to stop her money.

Three Years Ago

Andrew never forgot the first time he met Shannon. It was on the first day of his new job as an art administrator for a charity. He normally always felt nervous on his first day, but this company had been brilliant at making him feel comfortable.

The work was easy, if not too challenging. His job was to process applications from budding visual artists who were looking for funding for their projects. Since Andrew was an artist himself, it was the perfect job to have straight out of university. Andrew was earning money while at the same time, he was in the perfect environment to learn how to promote his own work. The management team was used to artists working for them and encouraged self-development as much as possible.

Andrew was pleased life was going great. The previous week, he had found a flat in Notting Hill and with Kadisa getting a job as well, life couldn't be better. The way things were going, it would only be a matter of time before he could proceed with his plan to propose to her.

He had been returning home late from work after being invited for drinks with his new work colleagues, when he first bumped into Shannon.

Turning into his new flat, Andrew reminded himself that although he appreciated the suit his mother had bought him, no one at the job wore suits. The next day, he would make a point to dress down a bit. To his surprise, he then saw Shannon, sprawled out on the steps of her flat. Her makeup was badly smudged and she was wearing a pink mini dress which was hitched up to her waist, showing off a black thong. She had one shoe on her foot and the other one was a few inches away. Her handbag lay beside her, the contents spilt on the floor. She was laughing uncontrollably; drunk. Andrew didn't know what to do. He briefly entertained the idea of turning around; perhaps he could find a pub or restaurant where he could sit for a few hours, until she might be gone. However, he was tired and wanted to be fresh for work the next day. He reasoned that because his entrance was different from hers, he could just quickly walk straight past her and hope that she was in too much of a drunken stupor to notice him. Taking a deep breath, Andrew started his walk. Just as he passed her, he instantly regretted his decision.

"Oi, mate!"

Andrew Stopped.

"Are you the new bloke that's just moved in?"

"Yeah," replied Andrew, noticing that there was sick all over the front of her dress.

"Boy, you're good-looking. Play your cards right and it just might be your lucky night."

Andrew felt as if he was about to be sick.

"Well, nice to meet you," he said nervously, taking out his keys.

"I can't find my bloody keys!" wailed Shannon. "I'm locked out."

Andrew sighed. "Do you live alone?"

"Are you coming on to me?" she burped.

"No! I am so sorry, I just thought maybe someone could let you in," stuttered Andrew.

"Oh, well, the night is still young, innit," replied Shannon, winking. "Well, as it goes, I don't live on my own—unfortunately. I live with my children. Let me think, did I send them to the babysitter or not?"

Andrew watched in horror as Shannon started a conversation with herself, trying to retrace her steps.

"Fucking hell, I remember, they must be home. I didn't see the point of wasting good drinking money on a babysitter, when I was only going to be out for three hours, tops."

Why don't you just ring the bell?"

"Bloody hell, you are a genius! A fucking genius! Why didn't I think about that?"

Andrew watched as Shannon vainly struggled to get to her feet.

"Don't just stand there, help me!" she screamed.

Reluctantly, Andrew hauled her up to her feet, and after watching her miss the bell a few times, he pressed it himself. Andrew heard the sound of the window being opened and then he saw Lauren pop her head out.

"Mom?" she cried.

"Lauren, thank God!" slurred Shannon. "Open the bloody door, I've lost me keys."

Lauren shut the window as Shannon leaned on Andrew to steady herself. The strong stench of vomit made Andrew struggle for breath.

"What's your name?"

"Andrew."

"Nice name. I'm Shannon. Just come from work?"

"Yeah," replied Andrew.

"What do you?" Shannon asked flirtatiously.

"I work in art administration."

"Art Administrator sounds like a good job. Looks like we could be going places."

Thankfully, Lauren opened the door before Andrew had to think of a response.

"Mum, look at the state of you!"

"Shut up and let me pass." Then, looking at Andrew suggestively, "Up for coffee?"

Andrew was just about to reply when Shannon promptly threw up over his brand new suit.

Shannon's voice brought Andrew back to the present.

"Andrew, I want you to meet my boyfriend, Ansell. Ansell, this is Andrew, he lives downstairs."

"Alright, Brother!" greeted Ansell, holding out his fist.

Andrew touched it.

"Alright," replied Andrew, fighting to conceal his contempt for any man that would proudly claim this woman as a girlfriend. Andrew was thankful that he considered her beneath him, despite his dire financial situation. He had his mother to thank for that—she always said that people would judge you on who you associated with and told him to choose carefully.

"Ansell's taking us for breakfast and then to the shops to buy new trainers," piped the youngest boy. Andrew remembered his name was Harry. There were certain names, in Andrew's opinion, that were designed for when you were over seventy; *Harry* was one of them. Who the hell named their kids Harry in this day and age?

"Is that right?" replied Andrew.

"Ansell says we can have any pair we like," said Harry.

"It's alright for some," laughed Andrew.

"Yeah, we'd better get going before the shops get crowded," said Shannon, puffing on her cigarette. "See ya later."

"Okay," replied Andrew.

Andrew watched as Shannon and her kids piled into Ansell's Range Rover. He couldn't help wondering if there would ever be a day in his life where he would have a wife and family, and whether they would ever get to go shopping like that.

Saturday, 12:50 p.m.

It was a very productive morning. Andrew cleaned his flat, collected his clothes from the laundrette, and prepared something to eat. Satisfied with his work, Andrew sat down on his sofa-bed with a plate of leftover chicken and switched on the TV. The screen flickered for a couple of seconds, followed by a loud bang. Then it went blank.

"Fucking hell!" screamed Andrew.

He instantly knew the television was beyond repair. Andrew had bought the TV from a local second-hand electrical shop about seven months ago. Normally, they would at least last a year. He knew that if he had saved up his money and purchased a flat-screen TV, it would have worked out cheaper than all the second-hand ones he'd invested in. However, Andrew also realised that it was fruitless trying to save as there would always be a bill to pay.

Andrew consoled himself with the fact that at least his flat was clean. It was a simple studio flat, with a large room that served as a bedroom, living room and kitchen. He didn't have a stove; instead, he had a simple hotplate that was placed on top of a very cheap fridge. Depending on how he felt in the morning, he would sometimes fold up the sofa-bed. He entered the room via a separate hallway that had a bathroom at the far end. It wasn't the best living situation, but it was cheap and meant he could live on his own. Andrew was never a fan of living with roommates; he didn't understand that whole concept of sharing a living space with strangers.

With the option of watching TV no longer viable, Andrew had lost his appetite. Depressed, he went to sleep.

The combination of loud screaming, a squeaking mattress, and the loud banging of a wooden headboard woke Andrew up. Annoyed, Andrew looked at the time. It was 9 p.m. and Andrew could hear the sound of a male voice crying, "Come on, come on now!" The male voice was accompanied by the gentle moans of a female voice, which got louder and louder. As it got louder, the female voice started to resemble the neighing of a horse until suddenly there was a loud, piercing scream that seemed to go on forever.

Andrew was used to the sounds of sex from the neighbours above, but this was a Saturday. Saturday was not their normal night. Their normal routine was Monday, Tuesday and Thursday, right after EastEnders. Their ritual would begin by turning on the television too loud to watch EastEnders and then, within minutes of the music ending, their sexual antics would begin. It was the type of activity you would expect from a young couple, but Andrew was a little taken back to discover they were pensioners.

Edward and Charlotte Haverbrooke lived in the flat above Andrew. Along with Shannon, who lived on the top floor, they completed the three sets of tenants in the building. Retired, with a combination of inherited wealth and a financial portfolio from Edward's former life as a barrister and property investor, they were the perpetual good-time couple. Very active on the social scene, their life consisted of dinner parties, cruises, and holidays in far-flung places. They owned an impressive property portfolio, including a country estate in Surrey, a villa in the South of France and a penthouse in New York. The idea of renting a flat in Notting Hill was their own perverse idea of "being at one with the people".

Edward was a man in his mid to late seventies, with a good head of hair that many suspected to be a wig. He had a very dark tan and was in excellent physical shape. Edward loved to show off his physique by wearing t-shirts that were deliberately too tight for him.

Andrew had taken an instant dislike to Edward from the start. His natural sense of entitlement as a result of his inherited wealth made Andrew's stomach churn. It didn't help that when Andrew had first met Edward, he'd had the nerve to ask where he was really from, even though Andrew was a born and bred Londoner with a typical London accent. When Andrew had said his parents were both from Jamaica, Edward had given him that look he often got from older white English people of a certain class or foreigners that he'd met from time to time. Andrew resented this because he knew, had he been white, Edward would never have asked that question. What made it worse was that Edward thought it was funny to speak to him in a Jamaican accent. Andrew wanted to know what was wrong with this idiot; he had never even been to Jamaica.

Edward had taken to walking around wearing hoodies and trainers and often greeted Andrew with his fist outstretched, as if he expected him to fist bump him. Andrew always made a point of opening his hand and shaking his fist. Yet this did not seem to faze Edward, who would continue his patronizing attitude by asking about the latest grime or drill track. Worse still, he would sometimes sing some of the lyrics, aping what he thought were street mannerisms. Andrew refused to play along, deliberately mentioning an obscure classical artist and claiming this was the last thing that he had listened to. In Andrew's mind, though, the most insulting thing Edward had ever done was when he had asked if he knew where he could 'Score'. Andrew pretended that he didn't know what 'Score' meant. Edward's expression was a picture of surprise when Andrew asked if he was talking about the football results. When Edward pressed on by asking if he knew where to get any drugs, Andrew told him that he had never done them in his life and didn't have a clue where to get them.

Charlotte was a spritely sixty-seven-year-old lady with the body of someone twenty years younger. With her charming, flirtatious manner it was easy to imagine her breaking countless hearts in her youth. She'd never really had a profession, other than the occasional modelling job. Nowadays, she called herself a 'Life Coach'. She was often seen rushing around Notting Hill in her gym gear, trying to get to a class on time. If she wasn't in her active wear, she was fond of wearing miniskirts, showing off her well-toned legs. Andrew had to admit she was very attractive and to be fair, if he was going out with someone with that body, he'd probably be on top of her like a pneumatic drill.

Andrew turned on the radio. He often listened to Talk Radio but barely registered what was being said, using it mainly for company. He briefly considered taking a walk, but the idea of walking around on a Saturday night, watching other people enjoy themselves, did not appeal to him. He lay in bed, wondering how he was going to get through the next week. It was around 2 a.m. before he was able to fall asleep.

Sunday, 7:30 a.m.

Andrew loved the feeling of hot water splashing over his body; he was enjoying his shower and was in no hurry to get out. Taking some soap from the stand, he rubbed some of it on his chest and watched as the water sent the suds downwards off his body. Despite going to sleep late, Andrew had woken up at his usual time. His decision to have a shower had nothing to do with him planning to go anywhere; it was just something for him to do other than stay in bed all day.

Suddenly, the sound of the smoke alarm rang throughout the flat. In a panic, Andrew rushed out of the bathroom and into the main living area. It took no time for him to spot the offending article. He had put some toast in the toaster before jumping into the shower, and now it was stuck inside.

Andrew unplugged the toaster and opened the window wide. Remembering that he was naked, he quickly returned to the bathroom, wrapping one of his towels around himself. Taking a second towel into the living area, he frantically waved it under the smoke alarm. After what seemed like an eternity, the alarm stopped. Andrew was about to put another slice of bread in the toaster when he saw that the remaining slices were full of mould; why hadn't he noticed that before? He had just burned the last piece of bread in the house and he didn't have enough money to buy more. He gazed at the jar of pennies that sat on top of his cupboard. Shaking his head, he sat on his sofa bed, taking deep breaths. What now?

He started to weigh his options; he could start to count the pennies, to see if he had enough money to buy some bread. He already had around five pounds but this was meant to somehow see him through the week until pay day. He reminded himself that he only had one day's work next week, and he had to figure out what he would do for lunch—at least if he had bread, he could make a sandwich. He also had five pounds in his bank account; if he went into the bank personally, he could take four pounds out, leaving a pound in so that his account remained open. If he had been paid the thirty pounds that was owed to him, he wouldn't be in this mess.

Resigned to the idea that he would have to break his last five pounds and find time during the week to get to his bank, Andrew decided that he wasn't in a hurry to go to the shops. He just needed something to do. He decided that he would clean out the one chest of drawers that he hadn't touched the day before.

The chest of drawers contained a mixture of clothing and textbooks from university. Next to the chest of drawers was a stack of art equipment he no longer used. Andrew decided to open the chest of drawers and throw away anything that he no longer needed. He started by looking at his old textbooks— university seemed a century away, a fantasyland that had nothing to do with the grim reality of his life now. He was pulling out one of his old sketchbooks when suddenly, a photograph dropped out. It was a picture of himself and James, his best friend in university.

Andrew stared at the picture. James was a handsome, six-foot-tall white man that was dressed casually and that had a confident, easy-going smile. He was hugging the slightly more formally dressed Andrew, who looked stoic. They were an odd couple. James, the son of well-off parents; everything seemed to come so easy for him. Andrew, by comparison, was the son of a single mother from a council estate, who worked after school and weekends to help pay his fees. James had a succession of well-heeled girlfriends, of which Andrew had struggled to keep track of. Andrew had dated one girl throughout university, who he had planned to marry. Yet they were united in their love of art and their appreciation of each other's talents, and both of them had come up from London to study at Birmingham University. They had spent the bulk of their time together working on their art, watching the old *Star Trek* series, and planning for life after graduation, when James would get a job with his father's firm and Andrew would find work. Then they would plot a way to take the art world by storm. Upon graduation, James decided that taking the world by storm could wait; he was going to have a good time. He went off travelling for a year, whereas Andrew had no choice but to hunt for a job right away.

It had been years since university and as far as Andrew was aware, James was still travelling. He would get the occasional letter from him, saying that he was having so much fun. He simply took whatever jobs he could find to support himself and when he ran out of money—which was frequent— his parents would bail him out. When Andrew had last received a postcard from James, over nine months ago, he had been working in a kibbutz.

Andrew put the picture on top of the cupboard and started to look through his other books. To his delight, five pounds dropped out of one of the books. Those five pounds could have been a hundred as far as Andrew was concerned. Happy about his sudden riches, Andrew decided that he might as well treat himself to a coffee at the café. Even the thought of having to put up with Gladys' legendary rudeness didn't put him off. Maybe finding the five pounds was a sign of his luck finally turning around.

Sunday, 9:15 a.m.

As soon as Andrew entered the café, he noticed something different. Alfie stood behind the counter as usual, but instead of his suit, he wore chef's whites. All the tables were neatly arranged with silverware placed correctly upon them, along with elaborately folded napkins. The small table where the customers used to collect their silverware was now being used as a billboard and was full of pamphlets advertising various events around London. The professor sat in his usual spot, looking around with a bemused expression. Andrew also realised that the lingering smell of stale nicotine was absent.

Andrew wondered if the café had suddenly been bought out by new owners. After all, in this area, he was used to seeing businesses come and go. But Alfie was still there, so that didn't make sense unless part of the deal was that he had to stay on. He looked around for the annoying presence of Gladys, but she was nowhere to be seen.

Andrew walked up to the counter, looking Alfie up and down.

"What happened here?"

"Standards, my friend," replied Alfie. "Standards."

"Right. You're looking good, though."

"Do I detect a note of sarcasm, my friend?" replied Alfie. "What do you want?"

"Oookay," replied Andrew. "I'll have a cappuccino."

"Take a seat."

Andrew sat in his usual place, still looking around the café. The Saturday night crowd were their usual boisterous selves, but the football crowd seemed to be more polite than usual. With more and more customers piling in, Andrew couldn't remember the last time the café had been this busy on a Sunday. He spotted Beatrice; something about her looked different and he was trying to work out what that was. She held last year's copy of "The Stage" high so that people could see what she was reading. He suddenly realised why she looked different—she'd combed her hair. Pearl sat opposite a man who looked to be in his fifties, and they were having coffee together. He was dressed in a black suit; Andrew assumed he must be a client. As Andrew opened his newspaper, he heard an unfamiliar voice.

"Cappuccino?"

He looked up and it was as if he had been struck by lightning. Standing over him was a total vision of loveliness that completely took his breath away. A young lady, who was roughly twenty-five-years old. Her face, absent of makeup, was a picture of natural beauty. Her shiny blond hair was tied neatly into a bun and she wore the standard waitress outfit of a black shirt, black skirt, and a white apron. Her eyes—fierce, intelligent and with a hint of sadness—engulfed him as if he was the only person in the room.

Andrew managed to splutter out, "Err, yes. Thanks."

"You're welcome, sir. I've been told by the management that your coffee is on the house. We are also offering you a complimentary egg and bacon dish, if you'd like it."

53

"Really?" Andrew replied, confused.

"I understand that there was an incident that took place the last time you were here, so we would like to make up for that."

There was an amused look in her eyes. Andrew smiled, drinking in her beauty. Even the memory of Gladys' outrageous behaviour was not enough to stop him gazing at her, totally enchanted.

"Oh yes," replied Andrew. "I think I'll take you up on that offer, thank you."

"No problem." She walked away.

Andrew could detect an accent, but he couldn't place it; was it German, Russian or something else? For the first time in his life, Andrew now knew what love at first sight felt like. It was not something he had even believed in before. His natural caution had prevented him from thinking such a thing was possible. He understood lusting after someone. Notting Hill had a lot of pretty women and from time-to-time, he did lust after a fair share of them. But this was different and Andrew struggled to work out why. It wasn't just her natural beauty—she had something else. She had a charisma that was rarely seen in people and she stood out because of it.

The waitress returned with the dish of egg and bacon, served with two slices of white toast.

"Here you are, sir."

Andrew stared at the dish in front of him. The bacon was burnt to a crisp. The eggs, although scrambled, didn't quite look natural. Andrew wondered if they were the powdered eggs that some restaurants used to save money, but then he remembered that from the counter, he could watch as Alfie cooked them. Therefore, that couldn't be it. The toast was slightly burned and already buttered, which annoyed Andrew, who preferred to do that himself. Still, it was free.

"Thanks."

"You're very welcome, sir." She smiled at Andrew before walking off. He stared at her as she strolled back to the counter with an easy athletic grace. Andrew could tell even through the dowdy waitress outfit that this lady had an incredible body.

Sunday, 10:30 a.m.

Drinking his coffee, Andrew watched the waitress as she effortlessly served the customers. She was an excellent waitress; very professional and at the same time, possessing a sense of humour which customers seemed to respond to. Andrew wanted to know what had happened to Gladys, whether she was on one of her sick leaves or whether she had been fired. If she was fired, it was no more than she deserved. As far as Andrew was concerned, someone like her should never have been let loose on the public.

Pearl suddenly stood up, collecting the coffee cups to return them to the counter, but the waitress walked by and swiftly took them from her.

"I'll take those, miss," she said.

Pearl's look of surprise was there for everyone to see. Pearl's client dropped a few coins on the table and she looked at him in disgust.

"Give me your wallet!" Pearl exclaimed.

Meekly, her client handed the wallet to Pearl. She opened it, took out two twenty-pound notes, and then dropped them on the table.

"That waitress is working too hard for you to start coming over all cheap. You're a banker, for fuck's sake, you were one of the people that screwed up the economy and had the nerve to use my tax money to bail yourself out. You selfish, overrated prick, I've got a good mind to charge you an extra hundred quid for the blowjob. In fact, now that I think about it, I will. Come on."

Pearl then grabbed the client by the scruff of the neck and angrily dragged him out of the café.

Cliff bounced into the café carrying a bottle of rum, stopped short, and suddenly glared at the waitress. He then walked up to Alfie and gave him a quizzical look before watching the waitress's bottom as she bent down to pick up some tissues that had fallen to the floor.

After spending an hour in the café, Andrew left. He didn't want to go straight back to the flat, so he went for a walk around Portobello Road. It was a busy Sunday morning, with locals and tourists walking around in anticipation of the shops opening. Andrew couldn't get over how beautiful that waitress was. After an hour of walking around Portobello Road, Andrew returned to his flat. However, he found it very hard to think of anything else but the waitress. He prepared himself something to drink and then fell asleep.

It was 4.30 p.m. when Andrew woke up. He wondered if the waitress would ever work in the café again or if it was a one-off. What if he never saw her again? Quickly, Andrew rushed out of the flat and headed to the café. The plan was to just casually walk past and take a look at her again. However, when he arrived at the café it was packed with the football-watching crowd and Andrew couldn't see a thing. Worried that he might be taken as a stalker, Andrew reluctantly went home.

He was convinced that he had just seen the most beautiful woman he had ever seen in his life.

Monday, 8 a.m.

The sound of letters dropping into his mailbox interrupted Andrew as he prepared breakfast. It was a bank holiday Monday, so he wasn't expecting any post. He then remembered that the postman often made the mistake of dropping his mail into the flat above. He discreetly looked out of the window and watched Charlotte as she scurried up the stairs, wearing a black miniskirt, heels, and with her knickers in full view. He reminded himself that EastEnders would be on at 8 p.m. that evening and that he needed to make a point of leaving his flat just before it ended.

Andrew inspected the three letters he had received. One was from a real estate company, the second was from the TV licence company, and the final was from his mother. Years ago, when Andrew had graduated from university with a job, his mother had decided that it was time to leave the grim life of Britain and join her sister in Florida. Andrew remembered his mother saying that with the state of her health, she needed a bit of sunshine around her and she felt that she could not go back to Jamaica after all those years away. Andrew's pulse raced at the thought of what a total shit he'd been to his mother. Her last letter was months ago and he hadn't answered her yet.

Andrew put the letters down and decided to finish his breakfast. He wondered what his mother had to say this time. One thing he knew for certain was that the life he was living now—living in a dump with barely two pennies to rub together—was not the type of life she had wanted for her son. She had wanted him to make something of himself and she had worked two, sometimes three jobs to make sure that he had been able to go to university.

Andrew wondered if the café was open today. If so, should he take a risk and buy a cup of coffee, just to see if that girl was there again? Then again, why was he getting excited? After all, what would a girl like her see in someone like him?

Andrew found himself surprised that he was thinking about a relationship, especially after all he had gone through with Kadisa. The pain of that break-up still haunted him, even after all this time.

Picking up the letters, Andrew immediately ripped up the real estate letter and opened the TV licence one. Great news: the letter said that they were about to send his details to a collection agency. Andrew couldn't help but see the irony of it. His TV was broken and he was certainly not in a position to buy a new one, but he was going to be charged anyway.

Andrew opened his mother's letter.

"Hello Andrew,

How are things with you? I do hope they're fine. I just wanted you to know that things are well with me. The house is finally built. It's a three-bedroom house with two bathrooms and a lovely garden.

You haven't written in a while, so I am guessing that your art career is keeping you very busy. I am so proud of you, son. Do remember, I am your mother; it would be nice to hear from you. If you ever want to call me, my number is below.

Love you,

Mum

Andrew tried not to get overwhelmed with that familiar feeling of despair again, but he couldn't help it. What was the point of life? It was as if he was in quicksand and all his struggles were useless—he was just sinking deeper and deeper. He felt that he'd really let his mother down, as his life was a wreck. Andrew didn't know what to do; he just lay down and fell asleep.

Monday, 7.30 p.m.

Andrew jumped out of bed. Getting his bearings, he realised that the whole day was gone and he hadn't made a single call. The day was wasted. It wasn't the first time Andrew wondered if he suffered from depression, he'd read that feeling lethargic and sleeping for long periods was one of the traits. He had to admit to himself that could be the case, as he was spending large amounts of time alone and he couldn't think of anything he was particularly enthusiastic about. Andrew lived a life where he felt constantly on edge, worried that yet again something else might go wrong, and it was draining. Yet as bad as his life was he didn't feel suicidal, so at least that should count for something. He was still upset about the letter from his mother, but if there was any chance of his life improving, he simply had to follow up on his plans.

Andrew heard the TV switch on from the flat upstairs. EastEnders was due to start soon. Realising what was about to happen, Andrew quickly put his jacket on and bolted out the door.

He was halfway up the road when he realised that he hadn't eaten anything since breakfast and was quite hungry. He couldn't face going back to his flat, so he continued walking and turned into Kensington Park Road.

The letter from his mother had affected him more than he realised; he was ashamed of where he was. What would she say if she knew what had happened? His mother was a driven woman and expected big things from him. She wasn't educated, not in the standard sense at least, but her life experience had taught her that you had to work hard to achieve anything. She had worked as a nanny and a cleaner. She had taken whatever shifts she could, just to keep them afloat. Andrew had to not only study hard, but also to surround himself with suitable friends. He had managed to do the first part very well, but never did the second part quite right. The balance of studying and working after school and weekends did not seem to lend itself to lasting friendships. His mother saw James as a joke but thought that perhaps by virtue of who he was, he might have contacts that would prove useful to Andrew in the long run.

As for Kadisa, she had disliked her even before she had met her. As far as his mother was concerned, Andrew was too good to go out with a girl with a "ghetto name". She always warned him to stay away from girls with names like Taniqua, Tiara or Alesha, because they tended to come from dysfunctional families and had behavioural problems. She reckoned they would eventually end up living on benefits and have kids by multiple fathers before the age of eighteen. She said she hadn't given him the name Andrew so that he could end up wearing hoodies, speaking broken English, and not have the manners to look anyone in the eye. Kadisa may not have been the right person for Andrew, but he struggled to believe it had anything to do with her name.

Andrew's main memory of his father was the smell of cigarettes and alcohol which, on occasions, was mixed with the smell of perfume. Andrew later realised that this must have belonged to another woman. He remembered a man with a lackadaisical attitude to life; his main priority was to have a good time with friends. He made a decent living as a carpenter and when he wasn't working, he was either at a pub or in the bookies. Come the weekend, he would party on Friday and Saturday night, only to reserve Sunday for sleeping all day so that he could resume the same routine again.

Andrew's mother had hated the fact that his father wasted his money on having a good time. Why couldn't he save his money? She couldn't understand his obsession with buying rounds of drinks for his mates, or why he had to attend every party they held; she couldn't see any of them being around when the chips were down. As far as she was concerned, England was not the place for black people to smile and play the fool. He needed to be focussed, work hard, save, and build something. In short, he needed to "fix-up," fast. She warned him that he needed to be serious and told him that only rich people had the time to play around. He never listened.

For his mother, the final straw came when his father finished work early one day and came home very drunk after being with his friends. Andrew had been happily drawing a picture of a car, when his father had laughed at it, claiming he could do much better than that. This caused Andrew to burst out crying. He then shouted at Andrew for not being man enough to take constructive criticism and wailed at his mother for raising a sissy for a son. Fuming, Andrew's mother waited until he went to work the next day, then threw out all his belongings and changed the locks. When Andrew's father returned from work, he stared at all his possessions scattered all over the street, then tried to enter the flat. When he found he couldn't get in, he just shrugged his shoulders, picked up his belongings, and left Andrew's life forever.

Walking past a series of restaurants, Andrew suddenly stopped at one of them and watched as people enjoyed their dinner. His attention was fixed on a particular table of eight, where a waiter was enjoying a joke with them. Andrew wondered if there was anyone in that group that had ever gone through what he was experiencing now. They all seemed so happy. It seemed such a long time ago since he was last out on a night like that.

There had been a time at university when James had persuaded him to go out for a pub lunch with a few of his friends. However, he had found the combination of drunken people and banal discussion not to his liking. In university, his life mainly consisted of studying and working. Kadisa used to say he had to let his hair down once in a while. However, Andrew hadn't wanted to be like his father and as far as he was concerned, the purpose of university was to study and work; that's exactly what he intended to do. It wasn't in him to get drunk like a lot of students he knew—he didn't even like the taste of beer and couldn't see what all the fuss was about. Andrew had a theory that liking the taste of beer was some sort of bizarre rite of passage that kids felt they had to go through on the way to becoming an adult. It was as if once you showed signs of being able to grow your own facial hair, you now had to—Ugh!—like beer. Andrew had wanted no part of that lifestyle; he'd had better things to do.

Lost in his thoughts, Andrew was surprised by how quickly he had gotten to the top of Notting Hill. He worked out that by now, Edward and Charlotte would be getting ready for their sex session. He stared at the Gate Cinema; if only he had enough money to treat himself to a movie. Andrew decided to walk back down Portobello Road, as he wanted to time it right so that by the time he returned home, Edward and Charlotte would be finished.

The night air was cool and it started to rain slightly. Andrew stopped in front of the Electric Cinema, one of the many features along Portobello Road. Punters were queuing outside and it looked as if there was some sort of special event taking place. There was a red carpet placed outside and several camera crews were standing on either side of it. Well-dressed people were walking in as others looked on. Andrew felt it was too much to imagine that he would ever be invited to anything like that. A couple in their mid-thirties—the man dressed in a tux and the lady in a gown—kissed passionately beside the queue, oblivious to all around them. He wondered if he would ever be in that position again.

He stood in front of the café and found the blinds were pulled down. He thought about that waitress again. She was so beautiful. He wondered if the fates were teasing him by having her show up; just reminding him that he didn't deserve to be in a relationship. His tears surprised him. It was time to go home.

Andrew walked past a pop-up shop, the lights were still on even though it was closed. Outside, two staff members were chatting happily next to a crate of stock. Andrew's stomach rumbled, he had to get something to eat.

"Hey, Spock!"

Andrew's body froze; he hadn't been called that in a long time. Andrew turned to the sound of the voice. Sitting on the floor, next to the supermarket

ATM, was a brown-haired man around Andrew's age. His hair was uncombed, and he wore an old tracksuit. His right eye was missing and he smiled a huge gap-toothed smile. He sat on a piece of brown cardboard and next to him was a cup with a few coins in it. The stench of urine was overpowering. But there was no mistaking him; it was his friend from university.

"James?"

Monday, 8:45 p.m.

Andrew tried to reconcile his happy-go-lucky friend
with the wretched creature that sat in front of him.

"Well, aren't you going to say hello to your old
mate!" smiled James.

Andrew couldn't stop himself from looking at his
friend's missing eye.

"James?" he found himself stupidly repeating.

"Oh, this?" James pointed to his eye. "I had a
little disagreement with this bloody drunk
bodybuilder. I wish I could say the other bloke came
off worse."

"What happened?"

"Oh, that's a long story, Spock, old boy. You
know how it is: travel, drink, drugs, and women. It's
the lifestyle, mate. It does take its toll on you,"
smiled a gap-toothed James.

"What about your parents, can't they help you?"

"What about them? They disowned me, mate. As
far as they're concerned, I'm dead," replied James

"Oh no, I'm sorry."

Ashamed, Andrew realised that he wasn't in a
position to help James; he was barely holding it
together himself. He couldn't offer to take him in,
his place was too small. Also, selfishly, James stunk
to high heaven; Andrew was not in the frame of
mind to do a big clean up. Even if he overcame those
obstacles and took him in, James could have a
problem with drugs and he was not the best-qualified
person to deal with that, least of all as James was
unlikely to become better overnight. Andrew's
natural survival instincts were telling him that, like it
or not, James would have to fend for himself.

James somehow seemed to read his thoughts.

"You know something, Spock, I love life. It's a lot simpler now. There's no one hassling me to 'make something of myself' or to 'stop that art nonsense and work in a serious profession, young man'." He imitated the voice of his father perfectly. Then, using a feminine voice to mimic his mother, he said, "'But James, what will the neighbours think?' Andrew, you know what my parents were like. They were always pressuring me, trying to keep up with the Joneses. I don't have to worry about none of that bollocks anymore. As for women; they are lovely but they'll kill you, man, they will fucking kill you. This is a lot better. As long as I can scrounge a few pennies together, get something to eat and have a place to sleep, I'm cool. This is what life is really about, man: the basics. So I'm good man, very good."

"I'm sorry Kirk," Andrew surprised himself by calling James by his old nickname.

"No worries, mate," replied James. "Look, man, why don't you just piss off now? I'm getting into a real groove at the moment and you're going to ruin my mojo. I've got to make a living."

"Err, yeah!" replied Andrew, embarrassed.

"Spock!" called out James, as Andrew slowly edged away, "This is going to be my regular patch now, so we'll catch up soon."

"Sure!" replied Andrew. As he walked away, Andrew could hear James pleading for spare change to someone approaching the ATM.

Andrew was shocked; he simply couldn't believe what he had just seen.

James had been the golden boy: privileged background, good looking and smart. Andrew had envied his easy-going charm and his way with women. The girls all seemed to line up to date James, who struggled to remember all their names. As much as Andrew had loved Kadisa, he'd always wanted the experience of having the pick of the most gorgeous women in university. James had always had the knack of meeting an attractive woman in a restaurant, at the bus stop, or in a shop, having a chat with her, and then later boasting that he had slept with her. It never took him long to accomplish that goal either—on one occasion it only took him half an hour between meeting a woman and sleeping with her. Andrew never understood what happened between the moment James said 'hi' to a girl and the moment he slept with her. It was all so confusing to Andrew, who felt that to get a woman to sleep with you, you had to wine and dine them for weeks. With Kadisa, Andrew had never really gone after her. Looking back on things, it just seemed that she was suddenly wherever he was and over a period of time, things started to happen. Andrew wondered what it must be like to have that gift of the gab. It must have been an amazing feeling, knowing that you could chat up any girl you fancied and within a short space of time, you would be in bed with her. James had been a lucky guy in that sense and to Andrew's knowledge, he never seemed to strike out with anyone.

Andrew suddenly remembered a serious incident that took place in his final year of university. It was an act that was so out of character for James that Andrew thought about it for months. It was the day James tried to kill himself. It began when James suddenly announced that he was "In love". Andrew had met Ginny several times and she was just like

James; happy-go-lucky, with the same love of mischief. To Andrew's surprise though, James even stopped dating his other 'friends'. Suddenly, Ginny and James were together all the time and according to James, planning a life together. This had been too much for Andrew to take, simply because James didn't feel like the guy he knew anymore. Andrew couldn't believe that anyone could change so dramatically. Kadisa, never a fan of James at the best of times, hated Ginny for no other reason than she was Ginny. Kadisa was like that; if she didn't like someone, she just didn't like them, she needed no explanation. Ironically, that was a trait that Kadisa shared with Andrew's mother.

James and Ginny dated for a few months, and then out of the blue, she dumped him. Andrew never got the full story, but somehow guessed that Ginny was just like James in many ways and to her, James was just another guy. James took it hard and in a desperate attempt to win her back, slashed his wrists. Andrew only found out about it when he received a call from James' parents to say that he was in hospital. They never understood James' friendship with Andrew, but they respected Andrew's studiousness and hardworking nature. They even hoped that some of Andrew's attitude would rub off on their son. They also knew that if James was going to pull through, Andrew's friendship was going to be a big help. He remembered sitting in the hospital while James described the sense of loss he felt now that Ginny was out of his life. Andrew struggled to understand that feeling and at the same time, was grateful that he was in a stable relationship. He had no way of knowing that within nine months, he would understand that feeling of loss perfectly well.

70

James was in the hospital for a couple of days and once he was out, it was almost as if Ginny had never happened. He simply went back to his old ways. His recovery was so quick that even Andrew began to dismiss the whole incident as just one of those things.

Andrew now wondered if that was the beginning of a downward spiral for James. Andrew should have known, because although James seemed the same, they didn't meet up to draw as much anymore and even when they did, James' art seemed to take a darker tone. His work became more and more abstract and he became obsessed with the themes of death and mysticism. In hindsight, Andrew realised he should have insisted that James saw a counsellor. Guilt overcame Andrew. He had let his friend down, and his current situation was partly his fault.

After university, with Andrew now worried about getting a job as soon as possible to start paying back his loans, James suddenly declared that he wasn't going to join up with his father's firm right away, saying that he wanted to travel. The decision surprised Andrew because although James had issues with his parents, he had always reluctantly accepted that his fate was to join his father's firm. But then Andrew had reasoned that this was what James' social group did—take a gap year. It wasn't that unusual. It was something Andrew would have loved to have done but he couldn't afford it. At least James had his parents' support; they saw seeing the world as something young people should do and they hoped that the experience would help him mature.

Seeing him again, Andrew realised that James had probably never gotten over what had happened with Ginny. Ginny had the same callous attitude towards relationships and sex that James had possessed before he had met her: that you could sleep with as many people as you wanted without thinking of the consequences to them. Andrew thought it was weird how people could go out, have a one-night-stand, and then simply have it be 'one of those things'. He didn't understand the concept of 'It was just sex'. Surely it was a self-esteem thing, perhaps neither party thought that they were worthy of being in a relationship? As far as Andrew was concerned, people with that disposable attitude towards relationships tended to have emotional scars of some sort. They were the type of complicated people that he felt it was better to avoid. He had lost count of the times an ex-girlfriend of James would seek Andrew out just to plead with him to talk James into taking them back. Andrew hated the sight of a woman crying her eyes out because what she had seen as a relationship, James had seen as 'just sex'. In a way, as much as he hated to admit it, what happened to James was simply karma; he could never really blame Ginny for her attitude.

Andrew now understood what James meant when he had said he felt this massive hole in his heart. Andrew had felt the same way when Kadisa ended it with him. The hurt and shock were so overwhelming, he actually thought he would die. He lost all motivation to do anything, staying in bed for days on end, and running-up huge phone bills by calling the psychic helplines. He had hoped they would tell him that Kadisa was going through a phase and that they would get back together. With one or two exceptions, they all said it would never happen. Then he discovered the Samaritans and hoped that by speaking to them, he could get things off his chest. The depression caused by the break-up was one of the worst things to ever happen to him in his life.

The timing of the break-up couldn't have come at a worse time for Andrew. Funding cuts had impacted on his company, and Andrew had suddenly been made redundant. It was sadly the usual scenario of last hired, first to be let go. Andrew had found himself needing to find another job, and when that didn't happen right away, Andrew realised he was in a desperate situation where he had to scale down his expenses. Things like having a landline as well as a mobile phone didn't make sense. After getting rid of the landline, Andrew decided to get rid of his contract smartphone and find the cheapest phone he could on pay-as-you-go. As time went on, he found himself getting rid of more things to cut costs. With his life caught in a continuous downward spiral, despair took over and Andrew felt more and more lost, as if he had no control over his life.

Looking at how his behaviour changed from being practical to lacking motivation and running up a series of debts by calling expensive psychic chat lines, Andrew could now understand how people became homeless. Andrew had often heard stories of people having reasonably good lives and then, through a series of incidents, ending up wandering the streets. It was not hard to imagine how a mental breakdown could cause someone to go off the rails. During his time living in the Notting Hill area, he had noticed one or two people who seemed normal but then, later on, they were begging on the streets. Andrew read stories of people that would suddenly walk out of their homes and vanish, only to be found months or even years later, wandering the streets, homeless. Andrew no longer thought that was so far-fetched. Life was showing him that it was a reality.

Andrew felt that a lot of people were just one unpaid bill away from homelessness. Most people never think about life like that, but perhaps that's the reality we have to face. Andrew had to stop feeling sorry for himself. Although he was upset by his mother's letter and life in general, no matter what, he should have made those calls. Although he hadn't, tomorrow was another day. As he only had one day's work coming up, he was going to have to hustle to get more. In fact, he was determined to get his life on track.

PART TWO

Evans Consultancy

Andrew sat in the very modern reception area of Kane Publishing. There were two large televisions, elevated on either side of the room. One was showing the BBC News channel and the other was showing videos and photos of the company's activities. There was also a brick wall at the back, which had an artificial fireplace and books on display nearby. This gave the place a cosy feeling, as if it was someone's home.

There was a black security guard with a strong African accent sitting at the reception desk. He was giving directions to a caller on the phone, who seemed to be having difficulty finding the office. Andrew could hear the security guard repeating the same information over and over again. He felt the security guard demonstrated an incredible amount of patience and wondered whether he could have displayed such tolerance in that position.

Even though Andrew had been temping for the last few years, he was still surprised to feel that mixture of impatience and nervousness whenever he started a new assignment. He had arrived ten minutes before his appointed time, which had proved to be a good idea because the office was located on the eleventh floor. Andrew was required to sign in at the ground floor security desk and wait until the security guard was able to contact someone before he was allowed to go up. Even so, by the time he got to the reception area, he was still at least seven minutes early for work. He had no reason to feel that nervous, especially as the job didn't sound that difficult; it was just putting together a series of publicity packs.

This was the second job Andrew had been given by this agency; the first was six months ago. Initially, Andrew had been very hesitant to take this job. It was only for one day, and a Tuesday as well. In Andrew's experience, if you got a job that was for just one day, it was very unlikely that you would get another job for the rest of the week. Agencies booked work for the whole week if they could; taking this job meant Andrew now had to pray that somehow, somewhere, someone would call in sick during the week and that an agency would contact him. He had to admit it had happened before, but Andrew was realistic and knew this may well be the only job he was going to get this week. He could only hope the following week would be better. Andrew took this job simply because there was nothing else on offer and reasoned that after the bank holiday, businesses tended to have a slow start anyway.

Signing up for this agency had been the easiest experience for Andrew; all he had to do was to provide proof that he could work in the UK, along with his name, address and contact details. There was none of that endless form-filling, taking numerous tests which had nothing to do with the menial work he was about to get, or the endless jumping through hoops that people called 'interviews'. Agnes Evans, who ran the agency, had told him that she could tell if someone was going to be a good employee just by looking them in the eyes. She was totally down the line with Andrew and told him that she couldn't promise him a lot of work, but if he did well, she would move heaven and earth to keep him working. Andrew had appreciated her straightforwardness, so he had to admit that after getting the first job, he was a little disappointed that he hadn't heard from her again. As far as he knew, his manager had been very impressed with him and had sent the agency a glowing report. Andrew reasoned it was just one of those things, and decided to keep signing up to agencies and looking for work. The call for the job at Kane Publishing came out of the blue.

Andrew liked Agnes a lot. She was a very energetic lady in her late sixties, with a stern demeanour that masked an individual that didn't just care about the job, but people in general. Her husband had started the agency many years ago; she had helped as both the accountant and secretary. When her husband died, she kept the agency on, only as something to do. Her husband had been a very shrewd businessman, leaving her assets and a considerable sum of money which meant she didn't have to work. Agnes said that, although at some point she would consider retiring, running the agency was something she simply enjoyed, and she planned to continue doing it for as long as she could. The agency was a one-man job, but every so often she would get help from her son, who loved her dearly and only wanted her to take it easy after a life of hard work.

The Temp Game

Dealing with Agnes was a refreshing change from the numerous agencies that Andrew also worked for. These agencies were mainly motivated by profit. The needs of their employees were considered far less important than the idea of making as much money as possible.

The major representation of this ethic was an agency called *Boost;* it was also the agency that gave Andrew the most work. Boost was a strange name for an agency as far as Andrew was concerned. It certainly did not 'boost' his enthusiasm for the work. In fact, in Andrew's mind, it would have been more appropriate to change the name to "Boast"*,* which was what they seemed to do best.

Boost carried the mission statement of 'Paying special attention to our clients' needs, with skilled, enthusiastic staff that are ready to go the extra mile'. In reality, Andrew saw them as a bunch of corporate leeches that would do anything for money. Visiting the office was like watching a bad episode of *The Apprentice,* with staff prancing around the place, screaming meaningless business jargon into their mobile phones. Andrew was convinced that excessive jargon speak was a typical trait of those that lived a shallow lifestyle and possessed limited intelligence. The men were suited idiots who loved to hang out in pubs and bars during their spare time, whilst the women wore high heels, expensive designer wear, and only seemed to talk about their next expensive holiday.

Andrew's booker, Katherine, was the epitome of that style: very attractive, impeccably dressed. She was the type of woman that had the habit of sitting down and crossing her legs in such a way that one could see all the way up her dress. This added to Andrew's sexual frustrations as he knew that as much as he would love to sleep with her, any attempt at meaningful conversation would result in him wanting to kill her. Katherine's main concern was her bank balance and after that, it was the next party, holiday, or night out on 'the lash' with the girls. As far as Andrew was concerned, the only differences between Katherine and Shannon were that not only was Katherine attractive, but she worked.

Katherine didn't seem to care about anyone who worked for her at all and treated all her temps with total disdain. After all, she was the one with the power to give them work. All she cared about was filling in bookings, no matter what it took. Andrew was often thrown into assignments that he was not suited for, in the hope that somehow he would be able to manage. Or worse, Andrew would be told that a job was going to be so much fun, only for it to turn out to be as dull as dishwater. In the past, Andrew had expressed annoyance at not getting an accurate brief of the assignments. The nasty personality hidden underneath the endless legs and perfectly manicured nails would come out, suggesting that behind Andrew, many other desperate souls were crying out to take his place. In other words, you either liked it or lumped it.

The other main source of income for Andrew was another agency called *Axis Recruitment*. They had an even lower pay rate than Boost and if they could, they would pay him even lower than that. Andrew often took jobs with them out of desperation. However, he hated the fact that he always had to argue for the right salary and then, once he'd done the work, always had a problem with getting paid. Every pay-day he would check his bank account with some trepidation, knowing that nine times out of ten, some administrative error would result in no money being put into his account and that he would end up having to chase payment. As a result, Andrew developed a sense of paranoia, always sensing that the worst was about to happen when he checked his account on pay day. It was a paranoia that never left him.

Andrew wished he had a full-time job, but it wasn't for want of trying. He had gone to countless interviews, sent off numerous CVs, but with no luck at all. It was all some sort of organised madness: learning interview skills, perfecting his CVs, jumping through hoops during the interview process. Job hunting was like being a hamster, constantly putting in all this effort but getting nowhere. It got to the point where he was sick of being interviewed by some snotty-nosed private school person who didn't know much more than he did. Time and time again he saw jobs advertised which he felt he could do, only to be rejected after the interview. On one such occasion, he bumped into the individual who had been given the job he was interviewed for. No way was this man as intelligent or as hard-working as he was; the interview process was all a sham. He had all but given up on getting a job in the conventional way. He felt it was like a lottery that he had no chance of winning. He reasoned that the only option available to him was to work hard as a temp and hope that perhaps someone would like him and give him a permanent job. In the early days, when he had first started to temp, if he was offered a job, he would refuse, explaining that he didn't want a permanent job in case his art career took off. Now, after struggling to survive for so long and having long since given up on his art, Andrew would certainly be grateful of a job offer.

Kane Publishing

Now, sitting in the reception area of Kane Publishing, Andrew reflected on his life as a temp and the numerous agencies he had worked for. He felt like it was some sort of a Groundhog Day experience, as he had lost count of how many reception areas he'd sat in, waiting, wondering what type of assignment it would be, who he would meet, and whether or not he was going to enjoy it. Still, this job was only for a day. If it turned out to be a bad experience, he could at least put up with it and think about the money, however little it was.

Andrew was given an information pamphlet from the security guard and read it with interest. The company was started ten years ago by an entrepreneur that didn't know much about publishing but, having successfully built several businesses, wanted to see if he could succeed in an industry he knew nothing about. He had been very inspired by a tragic event in a friend's life that had made him realise there were several reasons why people couldn't work: having children, being a carer, or by being over a certain age. Even though the last one meant that they often had a wealth of experience, it still didn't help them find a job. He wanted to run a company where those needs were addressed, where there were adequate support systems in place that helped with life balance issues. There were flexible hours available, a generous benefits package, and an on-site crèche for mothers, as well as a gym with a personal trainer and physiotherapist on hand. If a staff member needed to go to the doctors, they didn't have to make an evening appointment; they could go whenever they needed. The company performed well based on the philosophy that if you really cared about your employees, then good results would follow.

In the short time that Andrew was waiting in reception, he had seen two mothers come into work with their toddlers, who happily ran to the childminder without a backward glance, eager to take part in the number of activities planned for them.

Andrew remembered Agnes telling him that she had no time for badly run companies and that when he worked for her, he was accessing the companies as well. After his last assignment, as well as handing in his timesheet, he was required to fill out a company assessment form stating what he liked and disliked about the company. Agnes would not hesitate to drop clients if they mistreated her staff; her husband did not start the agency solely to make money, it was to provide a service for both employers and staff.

A smartly dressed pretty girl in her mid-twenties walked up to the reception desk, gave the security guard a fist pump, and shared a joke. He walked away; she smiled at Andrew and asked if he would like a cup of coffee. Gratefully, Andrew accepted.

He watched as she turned to a very sophisticated coffee machine behind the reception desk. Andrew was very impressed. Years of temping had taught him that if you wanted to know a company was good to work for, you took note of how quickly they offered you a drink. If they just shoved you into the job without offering you a drink, you were stuffed. It was probably not going to end well. But if they gave you a coffee and a chance to settle down, you were on a winner. Similarly, if the company had a great staffroom, then you were working for a good company, but if the staffroom was grotty and not well looked after, it was never going to be a great place to work.

As soon as the receptionist had given Andrew his coffee, a black woman entered the reception area. She was dressed in a dark blue suit, with a scarf of red, gold and green—the colours of the Jamaican flag—around her neck. This matched the headgear she wore. The padded shoulders of her jacket were like a throwback to the power dressing style of the eighties. She gestured to the receptionist and looked in Andrew's direction.

"Andrew Small?"

"Yes."

"Follow me."

Andrew followed as the lady spoke.

"My name is Marcia, did you have far to come?"

"Not really, I live near Ladbroke Grove, so it was just a matter of taking the Hammersmith and City Line to Liverpool Street." Andrew didn't feel it was a good idea to say how he had struggled to get breakfast that morning.

"A west London man?"

"I guess so."

Marcia led Andrew through an open plan area. Although there was a healthy mix of staff, the bulk of the employees seemed to be a combination of working parents, over-fifties, and retirees, with a few young people working as part of a mentoring program.

"First things first, I am going to show you one of the most important rooms in the building."

She led Andrew into a small kitchenette with a very sophisticated coffee machine and fridge. She opened the fridge to reveal that it was fully stocked with all manner of drinks.

'So far, this company seems to be well run,' thought Andrew.

"If you need a drink, just take. Do you want to top up your coffee?" asked Marcia.

"I'm fine," replied Andrew, impressed.

Marcia went on to show him around the building, including the crèche, where there must have been around thirty children ranging from toddlers to pre-nursery ages happily playing games with the childminders on hand. There was a mother dressed in business clothes who was casually breastfeeding her baby; she acknowledged Marcia as she walked past. Andrew could not believe this company. Even the gym was stocked with all the latest equipment and facilities you could need. Coming out of the gym, they bumped into an elderly man wearing a grey smock; he had a boxer's physique, a military bearing, and eyes that seemed to look right through you. Next to him was a North African boy in his late teens, also wearing the same coloured smock, with a large gold chain around his neck.

"Hello Marcia is this the temp?" the older man asked.

"Yes Indeed. Andrew, I want you to meet Peter Kane, he runs the mailroom," said Marcia.

"Nice to meet you," said Andrew, finding his hand being firmly shaken by an almost bone-crushing handshake.

"Likewise, mate," replied Peter. "This is Addy, he's doing work-study for me this week."

Addy nodded to both Marcia and Andrew.

"So, Charlie is still on holiday then?"

"Yep, the bugger is off for another two weeks after this."

"It's alright for some," replied Marcia.

"Yes indeed. Well, we'd better crack on. Nice to meet you mate, any problems, don't hesitate."

"Thanks," replied Andrew.

"Andrew, could you just bear with me a minute, I need to have a word with that young lady."

"No worries," replied Andrew, watching as Marcia walked up to the desk of a pretty typist and started a conversation.

Peter Kane and Addy stood behind a filing cabinet nearby, and Andrew couldn't help overhearing the conversation between them.

"Like I was saying, I don't care how you dress. In fact, you do look smart. But the truth is, some companies would find your way of dress intimidating."

"But that's not fair," replied Addy.

"Hey, I know, the world isn't fair and that's something you're going to have to deal with. There may well be a time in your life when you decide to get married and you will have kids to support. Then you'll need to put food on the table and the difference between whether or not that happens could very well depend on how you carry yourself. If you act like you do around your mates, that's not going to cut it, innit. Nobody cares how cool you are or whether you listen to that hip hop bollocks or that classical music shit. What it will come down to is how you present yourself and whether they feel they can trust you to do a job."

"But Mr Kane, it shouldn't really matter, providing I am qualified to do the job," replied Addy.

"In an ideal world, that should be the case, but it ain't. I've been around a long time, sonny. You'd better believe I have seen it all. It don't matter to me, you could be black, white, purple or pink. If I've got a job needs doing, I just want it done. But there are people out there that have never seen the likes of you, don't know jack about your culture, and nor do they want to. What they want is to feel comfortable around you. What that means for you, is that you've got to learn about them, understand their way of life and once in a while, although I know you don't drink, go to the pub with them. That's what you've got to do—play the game. It's not fair, it not right, and maybe in the future, it will be different; but in the meantime, tomorrow, lose the fucking chain."

Andrew sighed, watching as Peter Kane led Addy towards what looked like the accounts department.

Eventually, Marcia led Andrew to a medium-sized room where two middle-aged women sat behind desks. There was a third desk that Andrew assumed was for him. On the floor were various stacks of neatly piled publicity material. One of the women was black and the other was white, and they both smiled as Marcia introduced him.

"This is Donna," she pointed to the Black woman, "and this is Andi. Don't let them rough you up too badly. If they misbehave, call me; I'll whip them into shape for you."

The black lady made that sound that black people make, kissing her teeth loudly, while the white lady made a mock innocent face. Andrew smiled.

"We'll try not to damage him too much!" joked Andi.

"Good," replied Marcia. "Andrew, if you haven't got anything on this week, I will need you until next Monday. Is that okay?"

"Sure," replied Andrew, finding that he couldn't hide his look of relief.

"Good, I'll let you get on."

Donna and Andi

Overall, Andrew had a very good week. Although the work at Kane Publishing was extremely tedious, Donna and Andi's company made life there so much fun. Both ladies were long-term temps in their late fifties. Although they were from different cultures, they had a very warm and genuine liking for each other. Both were very professional and meticulous with their work but at the same time, made a point of having a lot of fun whilst doing it.

Andrew had a good feeling about the place as soon as Donna immediately asked him to do the drinks round. When he returned, Andi made a show of pounding the desk and making the drum roll sound as Donna dramatically took a sip of the tea. Donna swirled the drink around her mouth before swallowing, then gave a look of concentration before announcing:

"Taste's good. I like a man that can make a good cup of tea."

Andi pretended to wipe sweat from her forehead.

Donna Wilson was a good-looking single black mother. She was born in England to Jamaican parents and like a lot of people with Caribbean backgrounds, she had a habit of speaking good English but slipping into Jamaican patois from time-to-time. She was always impeccably turned out, paying particular attention to her hair and nails. She had a very lively personality and loved to have a laugh as she worked. Donna had two sons from different fathers. The oldest son was studying law at university and also worked part-time as an intern in a law firm. His father was a mild-mannered man who worked as a facilities manager at a media company. She admitted that he was the love of her life but with her habit of dating bad boys, she found his solid, trouble-free lifestyle a bit hard to take. He eventually married someone who was much quieter than Donna, which couldn't have been hard. Nowadays, they were good friends and seeing him happily married, Donna always felt a pang of regret. He was the one that got away. The second boy was of primary school age and was about to go to secondary school. She was constantly worried about him because of the company he was keeping. His father was in jail for murdering someone over a petty dispute in a night club, and the younger boy seemed to have inherited his father's nasty temper.

On Donna's desk was a picture of her current boyfriend. He was dressed in a bright red suit, with a purple shirt and yellow shoes; he stood next to a fancy car and looked like a cat that had got the cream. Donna told Andrew that he was an accountant who spent part of the year DJing in Ibiza.

Donna had worked at Kane Publishing for five years. Along with her job there, she also had several other businesses on the side: she was a hairdresser, ran a small catering business providing Caribbean food for events, and was a treasurer in a 'Partner'; a method of fundraising that people in the Caribbean community used. It involved several people putting money together, with one of them getting the full sum every month. During the early days, when West Indians arrived in Britain and found getting a loan from the bank to be a challenge, being part of a Partner was a way of getting the necessary funds to facilitate large projects, including getting on the property ladder. Helping Donna to manage her life was her best friend, Joyce, a stay-at-home mum, who also cooked for Donna's sons while Donna worked.

Andrea Dachauer, Andi for short, was a German actress who arrived in England in her late teens to study English. Andi was not pretty in the conventional sense, but with her handsome features and charisma, she had no problem attracting a lot of male company. Upon arriving in England, she met and fell in love with an up-and-coming English actor and ended up staying in the country. The relationship was a fiery one, with Andi often a victim of the actor's insecure rages. In the end, she left him and moved into a hostel for a time. Andi gained a love of acting and not only found that she was pretty good at it, but that she was able to build a small career from it. She did well, managing to get a few theatre roles as well as the odd film and TV part, the most prominent being her one line in an insurance company advert. Happily settled with a stage manager five years younger than herself, she kept herself busy with community theatre work as well as working on an alternate career as a writer of erotica.

Besides talking about their respective lives, which was quite lively, Donna and Andi loved to talk about television shows and films. They could spend hours debating which show was better; *Strictly Come Dancing* or *X-Factor*. The Perils of people on shows like *Love Island* and *Big Brother* were discussed with such an intense enthusiasm that Andrew thought it bordered on insanity.

At first, when Donna and Andi talked about the stars of these TV shows, Andrew, having never watched them himself, thought they were discussing people that they knew personally. When Andrew realised that this was not the case, he thought it was strange for people to get so engrossed in the lives of people on television—people who had no impact on their own lives at all. He also considered it was a waste of time.

One discussion that caused a heated argument was when Andi confessed to having a crush on Simon Cowell. Donna struggled to understand why any woman would have a crush on Simon Cowell rather than a real man. Cowell, in her mind, was a badly-dressed, talentless man who was full of himself. When Andi tried to defend Cowell, Donna raged, claiming that at least he should admit he was gay. Andi was not going to put up with that and went on to point out that Cowell was married with a son. Donna said that a lot of people in show business hid their sexuality by getting married. In this day and age, with society being more accepting, she couldn't understand why he didn't just admit he was gay, as nobody cared and hiding it made no sense. The argument raged on, with Andi pointing out that Donna was always looking for the worst in people. Andrew listened, hoping they wouldn't involve him in the discussion, as although he had never watched these programmes, he knew enough about them to be convinced that they were a fix. However, discussions like this were large parts of his working day, making him forget his own problems until he returned home.

On Friday, as it was pay day at last, Andrew looked forward to buying himself a sandwich. During the week, he had made sandwiches that were not always enjoyable, with some of them being just bread and butter. He planned to find himself the most secluded area in the staffroom and quietly eat it. With a slight bounce in his step, Andrew was just preparing to go out to the shop when Donna ordered him to stay where he was. She went out of the room and came back with two plates of rice, peas and jerk chicken, a slice of fried plantain, one German sausage, and two bottles of Dragon Stout on a tray.

"It's our Friday tradition," said Andi. "Donna prepares a meal for us. I supply the sausage; nothing like a German sausage. I can't stand English sausages—no flavour at all!"

"She's right about that, no flavour and too much grease. Yuck!" piped in Donna. "I remember going to a restaurant and watching them fry a sausage. There was so much oil in the frying pan, I was convinced the sausage was doing the backstroke. Or maybe it was the butterfly."

Donna did a comical expression of a sausage swimming, to howls of laughter.

"Oh," replied Andrew, as Donna popped out to get her own meal. "Are we allowed to drink alcohol on the job?" Andrew eyed the Dragon Stout, wondering how little he could politely sip before discreetly throwing away the rest.

"I should hope so," broke in Marcia, opening up the door with a bottle of Dragon Stout in her hand, "It's Friday."

Donna walked in with food for Marcia and herself.

"Hey, I notice you've given Andrew a bigger piece of chicken than your own boss," joked Marcia in a Jamaican accent.

"Go away from me!" laughed Donna.

Andrew enjoyed the best meal he'd had in ages.

Saturday, 7:45 a.m.

Andrew was surprised that Tesco was so busy on a Saturday morning. He had planned to start his shopping as early as possible to avoid the crowds; however, it seemed that the other shoppers had similar ideas.

Andrew was in a fairly good mood. He didn't have much money left over after paying his council tax and he only had work for Monday, but he wasn't going to let that worry him for a change. As Andrew finished paying for his groceries, he was surprised to see James standing gleefully at the entrance of the supermarket, accompanied by another homeless person that Andrew knew had been around the neighbourhood for years.

"Alright Spock!" shouted James.

"How's it going?" replied Andrew, looking at the other person, but still not able to come to grips with seeing his friend this way.

"Cool man. Hey Mike, this is my best mate, Andrew. Andrew, this is Mike."

"Hi Mike," said Andrew, grateful that his hands were full so he didn't have to shake Mike's hand.

"Alright Andrew, I recognise you from around the Grove, innit."

"Yes, that's right."

Andrew suddenly remembered that this was the guy that tended to park himself outside Ladbroke Grove tube station during the evening rush hour. In fact, on one occasion when Andrew had been coming home from work, Mike had approached him for money. Andrew angrily replied that he needed money too. Andrew wondered if Mike remembered that day.

"We lucked out. They've got baked beans on sale, two tins for 50p. Imagine that? We both looked at that and said, 'We're having that'."

Both Mike and James looked at each other and laughed. James was holding a plastic bag that contained at least six cans of beans, and he looked like he had just won the lottery.

"That's good to know," replied Andrew.

"What you up to, mate?

"Saturday chores." Andrew wondered if he would ever get over his awkwardness around James.

"Well, go on, hop to it! See you later."

"Right, see you then." Andrew hurried home.

Dropping off his groceries, Andrew took his clothes to the laundrette. The Jamaican man was rudely nudging someone who had the temerity to sit in his normal spot. The African man glared at Andrew as he put his clothes in the washing machine.

The laundry attendant announced at the top of her voice:

"You know, I don't think Donald Trump is racist at all, he's just saying things as they are." She stared at Andrew in anticipation.

Andrew shook his head as he walked out of the laundrette. He was definitely not going there.

Saturday, 8:20 a.m.

Reminiscing about work the previous week brought a smile to Andrew's face. With his clothes now in the laundrette, he decided to go to the café. He admitted that he was indulging himself. After all, his assignment would end on Monday and he didn't have anything on the horizon for the rest of the week. What was even worse, was that the money he was about to spend would have gone towards transport, which meant that even if he did have work after Monday, he would have to walk. Andrew didn't care; he was tired of constantly worrying about money and decided that he needed a treat. He remembered that the week before, Alfie had given him a free meal which was the cheapest thing on the menu; that awful-looking egg and bacon. He was going to treat himself to that.

As he was about to enter the café, Andrew spotted Shannon shouting at her youngest son, Harry. He sat on the floor, snot dribbling freely from his nose.

"Get up, you fucking little shit. I'm in a hurry."

The other boy, Shay, was calmly tossing his ball into the air. Lauren was looking slightly embarrassed by the whole scene, but as soon as she spotted Andrew, she just stared at him and gestured to her mother.

"Alright, mate?" Shannon broke into a smile. "Whatever you do, don't have fucking kids. I'm late for my hairdressing appointment and this little shit is pissing me right off."

"I'm hungry!" wailed Harry.

"Here, Lauren, run over to the sweet shop and get a pack of crisps. Fucking hell, Harry! You're gonna drive me to an early grave."

Once Harry saw Lauren running off at full pelt to the shop, he immediately stopped crying, satisfied. Swiftly, Shannon smacked him across the head.

"That's for fucking playing me."

Andrew watched as the force of the blow sent Harry staggering in pain and he immediately started to cry again. Andrew took that as a cue for him to leave.

"See you later."

"See you later, mate," replied Shannon, lighting a cigarette.

Andrew walked into the café and his heart skipped a beat when he saw the waitress carrying three plates to a group of customers. She was still there. Andrew couldn't believe it. There were times during the week that he had thought about her, but the antics of Donna and Andi had successfully kept him absorbed, ensuring that those times were few and far between. Andrew could recall seeing women in the past that he had thought were beautiful, only to see them on another occasion and realise that maybe it had been the outfit they had worn, their makeup, or even just his memory of them that had made them out to be more beautiful than they really were. Yet in this instance, this was not the case. The waitress was stunning.

The café was very busy. Smiling, the waitress pointed Andrew to the only empty seat available. Andrew sat down, still stunned that she was there for a second week. He wondered what the hell had happened to Gladys. Had Alfie actually fired her? If so, Andrew couldn't say he would miss her. Andrew stared at the waitress again and to his embarrassment, found himself sweating. The professor sat in his usual corner with his pot of tea neatly placed on a black napkin, his newspaper covering his face. He would peer out from behind it from time-to-time, just to watch what was happening. Bea sat at her table, a makeup tray placed in front of her, as she held a mirror up and stared at her tastefully made-up face. With her hair combed, Andrew was surprised to realise that she was quite attractive. Alfie stood at the counter, lining up the teas and coffees with a very burly market trader. Cliff was talking to him and watching the waitress.

The waitress approached Andrew with a smile.

"Can I help you, sir?"

"Yes, can I have egg and bacon please, with a cappuccino?"

"Certainly."

Andrew watched as the waitress took the order and handed it to Alfie. She then stepped behind the counter and seconds later, reappeared with a black plastic bag full of rubbish. With a catlike grace, she carried the bag out of the café.

Both Cliff and the market trader watched her bottom as she left the store.

"Alfie, you've done well there, me old son. She's fit. Where did you get her?" asked the market trader.

"Put an ad in the local paper, mate. She was the only one to apply. She even brought a CV and references."

"I tell you what, mate, it's good for business. She's given this place a major lift. Along with a lift down here," the market trader gestured to his groin, causing Alfie to laugh. "If Gladys doesn't want to work weekends, no great loss. It's brilliant to have a nice piece of crumpet to look at."

Alfie smiled.

Andrew didn't think anyone still used the term *Crumpet*. The waitress re-entered the café, ignoring the market trader's obvious leering. Picking up a plate from a table, she walked up to the counter and stared at Cliff's guitar.

"Do you actually play that or is it just for show?" she asked.

"For show?" exclaimed Cliff, indignant. "No, off course I play it."

"Play the arse, more like it," quipped the market trader.

"You keep quiet," replied Cliff as the market trader winked at the waitress. "I've been playing music my whole life," continued Cliff. "Back in Jamaica, they used to call me 'Sweet Mouth' and it wasn't just because of my way with the ladies."

"I thought it was because you had a sweet tooth or something," put in the market trader.

"Not Sweet tooth, man. Sweet mouth, my friend," replied Cliff, warming to the subject. "All because of my smooth, deep, velvety voice."

"Bloody hell!" smiled the market trader. "You're laying it on a bit thick, ain't ya?"

"Did you come to England to further your career then?" asked the waitress, genuinely curious.

"In a roundabout way," replied Cliff. "I came to England to further my life on earth."

"What?" exclaimed Alfie, looking away from the food he was preparing. "This is the first I'm hearing about this."

"Well, getting the girlfriend of one of Jamaica's toughest gangsters pregnant was not going to go down well, was it?" spoke Cliff, in that bragging manner of his. "It's a good thing I was good at cheating at poker or I wouldn't have been able to raise the fare to come here."

There was collective laughter. The waitress picked up another plate.

"So, did you learn your lesson not to sleep with someone else's woman?" asked Pearl, who was also listening to the story.

"Hell, no! How do you think I managed to buy my house? There were plenty of married women around willing to give me a little money to service them and keep the secret from their husbands. A man has to make a living," laughed Cliff.

No sooner had the laughter died down, then one of Pearl's clients burst through the door. Andrew recognised him from weeks ago, when Pearl had cheekily pinched his bottom as she walked out the door. He wore a dark suit, was sweating, and carried a bunch of flowers which he presented to Pearl.

"What are you doing here?" exclaimed Pearl, ignoring the flowers.

"I'm here to see you, Pearl," replied the man.

"Why?" replied Pearl.

"I had to see you," pleaded the man. "Don't you see, it all finally makes sense to me? It took me a while to get it, but I do, I really do."

"Now you're making me nervous, Chris. What is it?"

"I'm in love with you, Pearl," replied Chris.

"You what? For crying out loud, I've got a client coming in a few minutes!"

"That's just it! I want to take you away from all this stuff, build a proper life for you."

Pearl, suddenly aware that everyone in the café was watching the scene, started to scream hysterically.

"Alfie, Alfie, Get this lunatic away from me!"

Alfie hesitantly started to move towards Chris, who by now was in tears, pleading with Pearl.

"Pearl, you've got to believe me. I'm not here to cause any trouble."

"Get him away, Alfie."

"You heard the lady," spoke Alfie, now backed up by the market trader and Cliff. "She wants you to go."

"Okay, okay, I'll go," screamed Chris. "But it doesn't change the way I feel about you."

Just as Chris walked out, a tall, muscular, bodybuilder type walked in and headed to Pearl, who was just wiping a tear from her eye.

"Hi Pearl, You okay?"

"Fine, let's go!"

She grabbed her client and stormed out of the café. There was a collective sigh in the café as soon as she had left. The waitress walked over to Bea, who for some reason seemed to be very upset by the scene, and gently wiped the tears from her eyes with a tissue.

"It's okay. Now you don't want to mess up my make-up job, do you?" said the waitress.

Bea laughed, "You're right, you did such a good job."

"Thank you. Now you'll be able to do this yourself," smiled the waitress.

"But I don't have make-up," replied Bea, suddenly starting to panic.

"You do now, this is yours," smiled the waitress, pointing to the tray.

"But… I couldn't possibly take this."

You can and you will. I brought it especially for you," replied the waitress.

"Oh, bless you dear," replied Bea, tears coming to her eyes.

Picking up the tissue, the waitress handed it to Bea. "Come on silly, you're doing it again."

Bea took the tissue, genuinely moved.

The waitress walked up to the counter, then put Andrew's breakfast on the table with a sigh.

"It's all very exciting here, isn't it?"

Andrew smiled at her as she walked back to the counter. She was the most beautiful woman in the world and he now realised that he had fallen head over heels in love.

Interlude

It was a typical Saturday night in London's West End. There was an excitement in the air. People used to the restrictions of their nine-to-five jobs suddenly seemed to explode into life at the thought of relieving their stresses at the mercy of loud music and copious amount of alcohol and drugs. Tourists piled into the West End, eager to sample the delights of the London nightlife. And there was the noise— people were shouting at passers-by, hoping that some of them would stop to buy their wares. There was the traffic—the honking of horns, loud music blaring out from car windows. Then there were the squeals of excitement as partygoers hoped they might meet the love of their life. If not, a little casual sex wouldn't go amiss.

A long black limousine came to a halt right in front of a theatre. A black chauffeur sporting long dreadlocks and a smart dark uniform stepped out of the car, walked around to the passenger door, and opened it.

Andrew stepped out, dressed in a black tuxedo; he thanked the chauffeur and looked around, drinking in the atmosphere. He spotted a saxophone player dressed in jeans and trainers, playing a very bad version of *Summer Time*. Trying to compete with him nearby was a beatbox player, who used the microphone attached to the speaker and jumped around in order to take the attention away from the saxophone player. Andrew shrugged. He walked up to the entrance of the theatre; stood in front of him, wearing a sexy black dress, was the waitress. She smiled; Andrew returned the smile and they kissed.

He took her arm and they walked into the theatre together.

Andrew smiled at the thought for a moment, but only for a moment. He knew that it was only a fantasy and not based on any sort of reality. He already had made up his mind that despite his obvious shortage of funds, he would be at the café on Sunday, ordering the egg and bacon dish just to see her again.

Sunday, 8:30 a.m.

True to his promise, Andrew found himself sitting in the café with some egg and bacon in front of him, along with a coffee. Under the pretence of reading the newspaper, Andrew would take furtive glances at the waitress as she went about her work. He noticed her smile, the way she would look at everyone as if they were the most important person in the world, the way Bea seemed to have taken to her and was less agitated now.

As she moved around, Andrew could make out the outline of a thong underneath her dress. The thought of the thong covering her well-shaped derriere was enough to make Andrew quickly gobble up his breakfast and run back to his flat to pleasure himself with that image to sustain him.

Zungguzungguguzungguzeng

"Zungguzungguguzungguzeng!" screamed Donna, dancing around the room. The sound of the eighties Jamaican phenomenon, *Yellowman*, was blaring from the CD player. Andrew and Andi watched Donna as she executed a series of complex dance moves. Joining them was Donna's best friend, Joyce, who had popped in to visit. She was a dark-skinned lady with long, weaved-in blue hair. She was heavily made-up, wore fake eyelashes, extra-long nails, and lots of jewellery. She sat in the chair, dancing and twisting to the music, shouting out words of encouragement. On Donna's desk was half a Jamaican rum cake and an opened bottle of wine. Everyone had a glass.

"This is how we used to do it, back in the day!" cried Donna, wiggling her bum.

Andrew marvelled at how Donna's bottom seemed to have a life of its own.

"You know this tune, don't you Andy?" asked Donna.

"Of course," replied Andrew, recalling his mother's love of music. It was the one indulgence she allowed herself. She would spend any spare money she had on the latest sounds from Jamaica at the time; it was probably what initially attracted her to his father.

"What does Zungguzungguguzungguzeng mean?" asked Andi.

"I always wondered about that," added Andrew.

"Chile, do we have to break that down to you," laughed Joyce, shaking her head. Andrew wondered if there was some sort of a sexual connotation he was missing.

The first bars of Yellowman's *'Under Me'*, started to play. Donna dramatically paused in recognition of the song. Then she burst out into a *bogle*, a dance that was fashionable in the Caribbean community years ago. Andrew could feel the effects of the wine going to his head. At least with this song, the meaning was all too clear: Yellowman was singing about a woman underneath him, having sex. He got it. Then another thought came to Andrew's mind.

"That's what I don't get," spoke Andrew. "Yellowman was an albino which, from what I understand, was a big thing in Jamaica. He was constantly teased but the minute he had a hit record, he had to beat women off with a stick. How can people be so fickle?"

Donna and Joyce laughed.

"Something wrong with you, man. Yellowman has plenty of money," laughed Joyce.

"Wow!" Andrew shook his head. "But surely money isn't everything?"

Both Donna and Joyce looked at each other and laughed hysterically.

"Where do they get these people from?" asked Donna.

"I don't know. I blame the parents," replied Joyce.

"I don't understand. Surely a woman wants a man that loves her, with a strong sense of moral values?" asked Andrew.

Donna and Joyce roared with laughter. Andi looked on amused, sensing what was coming.

"Is he for real?" laughed Joyce.

"You're asking me?" quipped Donna.

"What is wrong with what I'm saying?"

"Andrew, a woman wants a sexy, rough, tough man; a man that can lift her up and sling her over his back," said Joyce.

Andrew couldn't imagine doing something like that. Knowing him, he'd probably hurt his back.

"That's right, he's got to have them lyrics too," Joyce went on. "If he ain't got the chat, he's not worth it. I love a man that can chat me up."

Andrew looked at Joyce, angrily wondering why any man in their right mind would make all that effort for her. She was extremely overweight with a gross personality. She actually thought that being reliant on excessive make-up, fake hair, fake eyelashes, and a large dollop of cheap perfume was the key to being considered attractive. Any man that even remotely liked her, would struggle to fight his way through all that cheap, tacky jewellery she wore.

"A man must be able to treat a woman in the manner she's accustomed to and he's definitely got to be a cocksman," Joyce went on, giving Donna a high five.

"Andrew, are you seeing anyone at the moment?" asked Donna.

"Well, no," replied Andrew.

"You know why? Because you're broke. That's right, no money, no honey," replied Joyce in a strong Jamaican accent.

Andrew's embarrassment rendered him speechless.

"Look, man," continued Donna. "You're not a bad-looking man, but your problem is you broke, you need a haircut, and you're a footer."

"A what?" exclaimed Andrew.

"A footer, man," replied Joyce. "You don't have a car."

"Footer, Footer!" exclaimed Donna, doing an exaggerated version of the old goosestep walk. "How you expect a woman to go on a date and still carry an Oyster Card?"

Andrew laughed despite his embarrassment. On the other hand, he couldn't help thinking that some of Donna's past problems with men could stem from her looking for the wrong qualities in them. Andrew felt that a lot of women had this hatred of men due to their own lack of judgement. In contrast, his experience with Kadisa didn't make him think women were the enemy. His doubts tended to stem from not only the fear of being hurt again but also, whether he felt he was worthy of being in a relationship in the first place.

"Innit tho," joined in Joyce. "Can you imagine going through all that effort of getting dressed up, just to go pon de tube? What a liberty!"

This was too much for Andrew, who felt like all his faults were being laid bare.

"Right mi pee," exclaimed Donna. "Give me a drum roll."

Joyce started to beat the desk, making a drum roll sound with her mouth.

"Look what I have here!" 'exclaimed Donna, dramatically pulling out a pair of electric hair clippers from her handbag," We can't afford to buy you a car, but we can do something about that disaster area you call 'hair'."

"You're joking!" cried Andrew, embarrassed. He always caught Donna looking at his hair, but didn't dream by any stretch of his imagination that she would bring clippers with her to cut it.

"No man, we don't want people saying you came to work with us and we allowed you to leave us looking like you don't have a home."

That remark struck a nerve for Andrew, as it made him think of his friend James and his own personal struggles.

"Trust me," put in Andi. "Let her get her way, it will be easier this way."

Andrew didn't know what to do. He was so embarrassed and for a moment, he entertained running out of the room. However, his practical side had to admit that having a haircut had been low on his list of priorities, mainly due to lack of money, so if Donna was willing to cut his hair for free, he wondered if he should take advantage of this. The fact that he would look a bit smarter the next time he went to the café was also on his mind. He'd definitely got his priorities wrong, he thought, as he should be thinking about looking smart for job interviews, not for a woman that would probably never give him the time of day.

Gleefully, Donna set to work, pulling out an entire styling kit. The phone rang and Andi answered it as Joyce watched Donna make a start.

"It's for you, Andrew," Andi handed Andrew the phone.

"Hello Andrew."

"Oh, hi Agnes," Andrew recognised the voice.

"There's a lot of noise in the background, what's going on?"

"The girls organized a little leaving do for me."

"It's alright for some," replied Agnes. "Listen, Andrew; I've got another job for you. It's two

111

weeks' work. I'm not sure if you would like it, but I thought I'd talk to you about it."

"Sure, I need the money," replied Andrew, watching as Donna put a mirror in front of his face.

"Well, the job starts tomorrow. It's with the same company, but it's in the mailroom."

Andrew pictured the image of Peter Kane. He remembered that the mailroom consisted of Peter, his cousin who was on holiday, and his grandson.

"Err, I see what you mean," replied Andrew, thinking how humiliating it would feel to be a graduate working in the post room. However, two weeks of work was two weeks of work, and he had nothing else going on.

"I'll take it!" announced Andrew.

"Good!" replied Agnes. "I've negotiated the same salary as before, so take down the details."

Andrew gestured to Andi for a piece of paper and pen, and then wrote down the details.

"It looks like you haven't got rid of me yet," announced Andrew. "Tomorrow, I'll be working in the post room."

The girls looked at each other.

"This is the last of the lot, mate!" said the burly black postman. He threw the sack on the floor, next to the others. Andrew counted at least twenty sacks of mail. Peter Kane picked up two of the sacks and dragged them over to Andrew's desk.

"Andrew, you can make a start on these."

"Okay," replied Andrew, grabbing one of the sacks and opening it up.

The post room was quite large and there were three desks; one for Peter Kane, one for his cousin, Charlie, who was on holiday and for whom Andrew was temporarily replacing, and one for Peter Kane's grandson, John.

Andrew's initial apprehension of working in the post room was quickly dispersed, as the job wasn't as bad as he'd thought. It was easy and straightforward, if not challenging; his job was to sort out the mail and then distribute it to staff. Later, Andrew would collect the outgoing mail, stamp it, and prepare it for posting.

Andrew initially thought he wasn't going to have a good time when, on the first day, Peter told him off for coming to work in soiled shoes. He was given a brush and shoe polish and made to clean them until it was done to Peter's satisfaction. It was at that point that Andrew noticed that both Peter and his grandson's shoes were spotless. Also, they wore a shirt, smart trousers, a tie, and cufflinks underneath the grey smocks that came as part of the uniform. From then on, Andrew wore his trainers to work as well as taking deodorant and moisturising cream. He made a point of going to work extra early so that he could change into his smart shoes and freshen-up before starting. He was expected to be exactly on time, keep his workstation spotless, and even stack the letters neatly in baskets when he was taking them to their respective departments. That being said, Andrew found that as long as the work was done to Peter's high standards, Peter was a fair boss and let him do whatever he wanted in his spare time.

When Andrew had told Donna and Andi that he would be working in the post room, the girls had taken it upon themselves to give him the heads up about Peter Kane.

Peter Kane was considered to be a tough old boot, with rumours circulating that in his youth he had been part of the old east end gang culture. He supposedly had friends amongst the most notorious gangs of that time, including the Kray brothers. After a short spell in jail for an assault charge, Peter had enrolled in the military.

It was in the military that he had met the company's founder's father and they had become firm friends. After leaving the military and finding it difficult to find a job, Peter had asked his newfound friend if he knew of anything. Peter was hired as his friend's bodyguard and chauffeur. When his friend died, the company was passed onto his son, who kept Peter on.

Peter went through a tough time when his wife, daughter and son-in-law died in a car accident, leaving their son John an orphan. His best friend's son had supported him during that time, allowing him as much time off as he needed to make the necessary arrangements, and so on. Peter now became his grandson's carer and had to face all the challenges that came with it.

Seeing what Peter was going through at that time, the company director was inspired to set up a company for the sole purpose of being there to encourage life balance. He wanted to ensure that staff never felt having a family was in any way a hindrance to making a living. Andrew was amazed that he hadn't realised the company was named after Peter, and thought that it was a wonderful tribute. Peter Kane was then asked to run the mailroom and security, with Peter bringing his cousin Charlie into work for him, as well as his grandson, John. Although mentally slow, John was a hard worker with a generous spirit. Not only did Peter run the security for the company, but also for the entire building. In fact, he created the team from a group of his old military buddies.

A Surprise Encounter

Andrew found walking to work was not as bad as he had originally thought it would be. The walk took him roughly two and a half hours to get to Liverpool Street, then another ten minutes to get to the office. Getting up extra early was not a problem for Andrew as he was an early riser and tended not to sleep very well anyway. However, he would arrive at work very tired and a combination of adrenaline and coffee kept him going throughout the day. He would thrust himself into his work as a way of forgetting his troubles and then, after work, the two and a half hour trip home was always daunting. Once he got home, he would get something to eat and go to bed so that he was ready to start the routine all over again the next day.

Andrew couldn't get over how much mail the company had to send out. This was particularly the case on the Wednesday, when Peter asked if he wouldn't mind staying an extra half an hour to help clear the backlog. Andrew agreed, knowing he needed the money.

As they left work, Andrew walked out of the office with John, who mentioned that he was going to Paddington and suggested that they could ride the train together. Andrew told him that sadly, he was meeting some friends to go out. He then walked in the opposite direction, stopping only to watch John head down to the tube station before changing his shoes and starting the long trek home.

It was 5:45 p.m.: Andrew calculated he would be home by roughly 7:15 p.m. Everywhere Andrew looked, masses of people were rushing home, footsteps pounding the pavements only to pause briefly to collect either a magazine or a local newspaper from one of the many street vendors. Large groups of people started to gather outside pubs. Men in suits stood in groups along with well-dressed women, some of whom were holding their cigarettes in that strange way; away from people, as if this would actually prevent the smoke from affecting them. The streets were filled with the strong scent of stale beer and the equally overpowering smell of cigarette smoke. As he walked, it seemed to Andrew that he was seeing the same scene over and over again: the same pub, the same people wearing the same boring corporate outfits, talking the same boring talk; the same people talking a little too loudly on their mobile phones; the same women wearing heels so tall that they were doing a remarkable impersonation of the leaning tower of Pisa. Not for the first time, Andrew wondered why anyone would aspire to work here— where they would have to endure travelling to work in overcrowded trains, working in stuffy offices, making money for someone else—unless, like him, they had no choice.

Andrew suddenly remembered that James had a friend that was exactly like that; Lance Styles. He had hated being a student and worse, he had hated being a *poor* student. Lance dreamt of the day when he could go into a pub and not only afford to buy a pint, but to treat his friends to one also. His poverty frustrated him so much that he had dropped out of university just so that he could work as an office junior. It was not hard to imagine Lance being one of those faceless people standing outside a pub with a pint in his hand, only for him to retire forty to fifty

117

years later. He would most likely be divorced and still paying off his ex-wife's mortgage so that she could continue to live in the house with his two children, who didn't respect him owing to his excessive drinking habits. He would probably have a gold watch to show for a lifetime of shuffling papers.

As Andrew continued his journey home, the streets started to fill up with people who were getting ready for a night on the town. Groups of men stormed the streets, making that guttural sound associated with football fans, all under the illusion that this was a cool thing to do. A group of women dressed in bunny outfits rushed past Andrew; he imagined it was a hen night. Andrew didn't see himself getting married but unless he was desperate, he swore he would never marry a woman who thought a hen night like that was a fun thing to do.

Watching all the activities around him, Andrew felt the same sense of isolation. Everything was happening around him but he was in this strange bubble, apart from everything; just an observer. He wondered if life was like his walk home—a feeling of endlessly walking without a real purpose or destination. Sure, he was going home, but what was all that about? He would wake up in the morning, only to do the same thing over and over again; what was the point? Was everyone just doing the same things endlessly, with no rhyme or reason? Walking like this, Andrew found that to stop feeling sorry for himself, he had to fantasize about having a better life. He would love to have a nice girlfriend and a nice place. He'd also love a car, especially after this walking experience. A car would be a dream.

After walking for a while, Andrew began to feel the familiar pangs of hunger. This was not surprising, since he was living off homemade sandwiches and the free coffee from Kane Publishing. He didn't have much money, but if he could get a packet of crisps, that would at least tide him over until he got home. He popped into a small shop selling groceries, but couldn't believe how expensive crisps were. Angrily, he walked out and found a supermarket, where prices were cheaper. Andrew quickly consumed the crisps, reasoning there was nothing better than Ready Salted. The other flavours were interesting but didn't do it in the way Ready Salted did. Wiping his mouth, he was shocked to see the waitress from the café across the street. Her shoulder-length hair was out, making her look even more beautiful. She wore black leggings with a black leather jacket and black boots. Even though she appeared to be in a hurry, she still moved with that amazing grace that had become so familiar.

Andrew's imagination ran into overdrive. He began having that fantasy where he was meeting her for a date in the theatre. Then he imagined what it would be like if his limousine was parked outside of the café; he would step out and tell her that she didn't have to work there anymore as he was taking her away.

His mother loved an old Richard Gere film, where Richard Gere's character rescues a girl from the factory. She would make Andrew watch that film over and over again. In Andrew's fantasy, all the regulars of the café would watch as he lifted the waitress in his arms and took her out. Andrew's imagination went into such an overdrive, that it carried him all the way home.

At work, every spare moment Andrew got would be spent wondering about this girl: was she a student, what was her name, where was she from? On Friday, he picked up a piece of blank photocopier paper and started to sketch her from memory. Just as he had completed his handiwork, the girls came to visit, carrying some food for him. The smell of the jerk chicken meal was a welcome one.

Andi noticed the picture and stared at it in admiration.

"That's really good, Andrew."

"Thanks," replied Andrew, wishing he had managed to hide it before the girls had arrived.

"She's very pretty," commented Donna. "Is she someone we know?"

"No, she's someone from a café I go to," replied Andrew.

The girls stared at Andrew as if seeing him for the first time.

"You are very talented," said Andi.

Andrew smiled shyly.

Ansell

It was 9:25 a.m. when Andrew woke up, which was surprising, given that he was generally an early riser. Despite his legs still hurting from his walk back and forth to work every day, Andrew had slept well. It was Saturday morning and Andrew started his normal routine of taking his clothes to the laundrette. Since his shouting session, he was glad when no one decided to talk to him; that suited him fine. Once he had been to the laundrette and had left his clothes there, he got a newspaper and headed to the café.

The café was busy. The professor sat in his usual spot, surveying the crowd. Cliff sat on a table, fast asleep. Pearl sat with a coffee in front of her. The waitress was taking coffee to the market trader, who was so busy leering at her that he didn't notice Bea giving him a dirty look.

As soon as Andrew had sat in his favoured position, the waitress sailed over to him and asked for his order. He ordered his usual meal and watched as the waitress seemed to glide to the counter.

Suddenly there was an ear-piercing scream. Andrew's eyes darted towards the direction of the sound and saw that it had come from the professor, who was squealing uncontrollably as a young couple sat at his table. The waitress futilely tried to calm the professor down as he jumped up and down, spittle gushing from his mouth. Alfie walked over to the young couple and moved them to another table. Instantly, the professor stopped, replacing his screams with gentle sobs. Alfie spent a few minutes talking to the professor, pouring some tea from the pot on the table and encouraging him to drink it.

With the professor calm, Alfie walked over to the waitress. She was visually shaken and watching as Alfie talked to her and gave her a quick hug, Andrew longed to rush over to her and hold her in his arms. It didn't take long before she was composed again and had returned to work as if nothing had happened.

'There's more drama at this café than in EastEnders,' thought Andrew. *'If Edward and Charlotte were here, they would be doing it on the tables.'*

Andrew was about to flick through his paper when a distraught Ansell strode through the café. There was a strong smell of alcohol as he walked up to the counter. Ansell ordered a cup of tea to take away and as soon as the waitress had given it to him, he turned to walk out of the café. Then he spotted Andrew.

"What's up, man?"

"Nothing much," replied Andrew.

Then, without another word, Ansell plopped himself on the seat opposite him and promptly burst into tears.

Stunned, Andrew didn't know what to do. The stench of alcohol was overpowering, Andrew suddenly noticed that people were looking in his direction. He was uncomfortable being the centre of attention—this was not exactly what he had in mind for his Saturday morning.

Ansell continued to blubber uncontrollably, picking up a napkin to blow his nose with a large honk, before continuing to sob. Andrew briefly considered moving to another table, but the café was crowded and there was nowhere else to go. He wondered if he could ask the waitress to put his food

122

in a doggy bag, but he was rooted to the spot. How was he going to get out of this?

"She's dumped me," Ansell burst out through his tears. "She's dumped me!"

Andrew stared at him, trying to hide the contempt he had for Ansell for actually going out with Shannon in the first place. As far as he was concerned, it sounded like a lucky escape. Andrew surprised himself by muttering:

"I'm sorry to hear that."

Andrew couldn't help but feel a sense of wonder that a huge muscular man could become an emotional wreck over a woman that he, even in his own impoverished state, would not touch with a barge pole.

"I don't understand what happened," continued Ansell, "I did everything for her. I took her out, gave her money for the kids, sorted out her flat. I loved her."

"I'm sorry," was all Andrew could find himself saying, hoping that Ansell wouldn't detect the insincerity in his voice.

"I don't understand women, you do all you can for them and then they still dump you."

That remark suddenly struck a chord with Andrew, as he remembered his relationship with Kadisa.

"I don't know," replied Andrew, as he wondered what Shannon had over these guys. Was she that good in bed? "I guess sometimes nice guys finish last."

"You think?" replied Ansell, making an annoying slurping noise with his tea.

"I don't know, I'm not exactly an expert on women."

123

Andrew remembered how devastated he had been over his relationship break-up, and then thought about what had happened to James. However, connecting with Ansell on that level did not prevent him from wishing Ansell would leave his table.

"So, where are you off to now?" asked Andrew, hoping Ansell would take the hint.

At that point, the waitress put Andrew's breakfast on the table.

"I don't know," replied Ansell, suddenly eyeing Andrew's food. "Err, excuse me, can I have a full English to stay please?"

"Sure," replied the waitress.

'Oh for fuck's sake,' thought Andrew.

"You know, I can believe how cheap the prices are in this café. It's mad, bro," spoke Ansell, making himself comfortable. "Totally mad."

"I know," replied Andrew, glumly.

"And they serve massive portions too, rude boy."

"Yeah."

"Man, it's really good to talk to you, bro," continued Ansell. "I always got the impression that you were a bit standoffish, you know. A bit of a snob, you know what I mean?"

Andrew wondered if this guy was doing a bad impression of how to win friends and influence people.

"But you're alright, a proper cool geezer."

"I guess I should take that as some kind of a compliment," said Andrew, whilst thinking to himself, *'Fucking prick.'*

Despite himself, Andrew couldn't help marvelling at Ansell's ability to alternate between a strong cockney accent and Jamaican patois, a common trait of blacks of West Indian descent. Andrew rarely did this, remembering his mother's insistence that he spoke the Queen's English, claiming he would never be treated with any respect if he didn't.

"Anyway, she ended it just like that, man, right out of the fucking blue. She said she needed more time to be with her kids. What a laugh! I was spending more time with her kids than she was. I took them to school, bought them clothes, even paid for swimming lessons. If the kids had problems with their teachers, I dealt with it. I was a proper father to them. It's the way she did it too. We were actually at the chippy at the time!"

"Oh!"

"Yeah, rude boy. I was treating her to a proper chippy supper, and she just ended it right there, in front of her kids."

"No way, in the chip shop!" replied Andrew. *'Classy idea,'* he thought to himself.

"Yeah, she made sure she waited until I'd paid for the dinner though."

Andrew admitted to himself that given the state of his finances, he could understand that being annoying.

"So what happened then? Did you leave the restaurant?" asked Andrew. Despite himself, he was getting interested in the story.

"Naah, man. I am a gentleman, rude boy. I made sure that they got home safely. I gave them a lift, tucked the kids in bed, gave her a couple of hundred quid to see her through the week, and then I left."

Andrew couldn't believe it—this guy was a bloody idiot. Shannon must have seen this buffoon coming a mile off. He was caught off-guard when

Ansell burst into tears once again. The waitress put Ansell's breakfast on the table with a wry smile and walked off.

With that, Ansell stopped crying and tucked into his food.

"This food may be cheap but it's good, man. Do you want some?" Ansell jabbed his fork into a sausage and offered it to Andrew.

"No, I'm good," replied Andrew, watching the waitress as she sat down to talk to Pearl, who seemed to be crying.

"She's fit, ain't she!" said Ansell.

"Which one?" asked Andrew.

"You know very well who I mean," replied Ansell, looking at him knowingly. "Don't get me wrong, mate, Pearl is fit, but the other one, she's on another level of fitness."

"What do you mean?" asked Andrew, trying to affect the air of nonchalance.

"Well, look at Pearl. If you look at her face carefully, she's not really that attractive. I'm not saying she's ugly, but if you took away all that over-the-top make-up, she's very bland-looking. She's the type of woman that if you were to look at her old school pictures, she just wouldn't have stood out."

"The thing is, bro," Ansell continued, leaning forward and looking from side to side. Andrew wondered why Ansell had to whisper so loudly. "Once puberty kicks in, and all of a sudden this bland-looking girl gets this kick-ass figure, things change. I mean, look at that body—look at that!" Ansell made a lustful sound, causing Andrew to blush. "Lord have mercy, that's a lethal weapon. You know, she puts in a lot of effort in the gym to keep it looking that good. I'm not even convinced that those tits are real. Women like her, you shag them just as an appreciation of all the hard work they put in whilst training.

"But she's not the type that you'd marry. Too vain, man. She's the type you see on the train or bus, spending the whole journey putting on makeup and still not looking that good. She's never going to look after you. Now, being ugly is not a bad thing. Some girls aren't pretty in the conventional way, but they've got that raw sexual magnetism that makes you want to give them one constantly. Back in the day—you're too young to know her—there was an actress called Ellen Barkin and she had that look. Boy, I had plenty of wet dreams over that one, let me tell you."

Andrew didn't know what to say.

"Now, the other one ... she stands out. She is just fit. You could tell that from the moment she popped out the womb. She was probably turning a lot of heads even then, but what makes her special is that she has a really nice nature too. You can tell. There are a lot of pretty girls that have that attitude, you must know what I mean, where they think they are too good for you to talk to. But that one there…"

Ansell gestured to the waitress.

"She's got none of that. It doesn't mean you can mess her about—no way! But she is genuine and everything about her is class. She's the type that if you had her on your arms, you could profile properly."

"Profile?" asked Andrew.

"You know, pose," replied Ansell. "Show her off. Have you ever dated a girl so gorgeous that everyone stares at you when you enter a room?"

Andrew couldn't say he had. He'd only had one semi-serious relationship before Kadisa. She had been okay-looking and Kadisa was pretty, so when he had gone out with either, he had been happy to be holding hands with them. But he understood what Ansell was talking about. In his fantasies, there were girls he dreamt about going on a date with; jaw-dropping stunners that could light up a room and make you feel ten feet tall just because they were with you. Anna was definitely that type—the girl of any man's dreams.

Ansell went on, "She fits the bill, mate. Totally down the line. You could take her to a celebrity party even in her waitress outfit and she'd still stand out among the other women. Even more important than that, she's the type that really would look after you. She's just got something, man. Definitely."

"Yeah."

"Yeah man, I recognise that look, bro."

"What look?"

"Don't worry bro, your secrets safe with me," spoke Ansell.

"What are you talking about?" asked Andrew.

"Come on, you know what I mean. You fancy her, don't you?" Ansell's laugh was a huge booming one that caused his massive body to shake.

"I don't," replied a flustered Andrew.

"Okay, be like that, bro," replied Ansell with a loud whisper. "I reckon she'd be brilliant in bed, man. You could really beat her up."

"I don't hit women," Andrew said, shocked.

"Nah man, I don't mean hit her, I mean beat her up." He simulated a jerking movement on his chair. "You could give her a good seeing to." He used a hand gesture and simulated an American accent,

128

"You could hide the salami." He started laughing uncontrollably.

Andrew felt like the earth could swallow him up whole. He was not the type of person to talk about women in this way. Ansell was such an uncouth clod.

"You never know," Ansell was in full flow now, "you might have a chance with her."

"I don't think—" Andrew suddenly stopped, realising that he was giving himself away.

"You know, nuff white women love the brothers, especially the foreign ladies. If you give them the chat, you'll be away. They all want a BMW."

"BMW?"

Yeah; A black man's woman."

As far as Andrew was concerned, Ansell was a thick tosser. If anything, Ansell was the type of black man that a lot of white women who didn't know any better would like. He was the muscular idiot with a happy-go-lucky personality that could attract women; not the intense, miserable, starving artist like himself.

One summer, Andrew had come upon an article describing how some Korean women loved going out with black men. It prompted Andrew to start watching online videos of women from various countries, talking about why they liked black men; it was an eye-opening experience. The reasons ranged from the standard comments about their bodies, to the fact that they danced well and didn't mind the fact that women were a bit fat. Andrew couldn't believe the amount of stereotypical ideas that still existed in this day and age. However, he noticed that none of them mentioned his own traits. Andrew worked out that women would be attracted to idiots like Ansell, but would soon outgrow them once the reality of life reared its ugly head. That was why, years later, Andrew observed so many mixed-race kids running around with white single mothers. The bubble simply burst.

"I tell you what," continued Ansell, "I can hook you up. Want me to put a good word in for you?"

"Nah, I'm good," replied Andrew, as he considered whether it would be worth putting his life at risk by telling him to fuck off. "Well, nice talking to you," Andrew got up. "I've got some clothes in the laundrette."

"Err, okay," a surprised Ansell replied. "Okay bro, hold it down. See you later."

Ansell held out his fist. Andrew touched it and fled the restaurant.

Saturday, 10:45 a.m.

Embarrassed and shaking, Andrew walked briskly to the laundrette. He noticed that his clothes had been taken out of the washing machine and put in a plastic basket, while the machine was spinning around with someone else's load. It was extremely busy in the laundrette so this didn't surprise Andrew; it was something he was used to and it often happened whenever he left his clothes in the machine for too long. As usual, he couldn't afford to dry all his clothes, so he picked out a few of them and put them in the dryer. He planned to hang the rest up in his flat. Once the clothes were dry, he placed them into a second bag and went back to his flat.

Andrew was uncomfortable with the fact that Ansell had worked out he had a crush on the waitress. He really hoped he wasn't the type of person to open his mouth. Unfortunately, he probably was. Andrew was so into his thoughts that he almost bumped into Shannon.

Shannon was standing near the entrance to the flat, wearing a black dress with slippers. Andrew thought it was a bit tacky and wondered if she had spent a lot of time dreaming up that tasteless look. Next to her was a very thin North African man, wearing shorts that showed off his skinny legs. He was holding Shay's hand.

"Watch where you're going, mate!" Sharon exclaimed. "Daydreaming again?"

"I'm sorry," replied Andrew, eyeing up the man.

"This is Yusuf," said Shannon.

"Nice to meet you, man." Yusuf extended his hand.

131

"Nice to meet you," replied Andrew, shaking his hand and wondering what Ansell was going to do if he found out. Some consolation for Ansell would be that if Yusuf managed to last six months, this would be considered long-term for Shannon.

Hours later, Andrew woke up after having a nap. He checked the time and found it was 3.30 p.m. He decided to make himself a cup of tea and put on a dance mix CD, one of many he had purchased from Portobello Market, back in the days when he'd had the money. He found listening to the radio very annoying due to the useless banter that radio hosts came out with. Combine that with the endless commercials, and it was not a pleasant experience. As such, he preferred his CDs. Andrew pressed the start button. At that point, the bell rang, which puzzled him as he wasn't expecting anyone. He opened the door and was surprised to see Ansell standing outside, a grin as wide as the Cheshire Cat on his face.

"Hi bruv, we had such a good chat, I thought I'd pay you a visit, innit."

Cheerfully, he walked in and looked around. Andrew decided that despite his hatred of the gym, he would gladly train 24/7 just so that he could be big enough to kick this idiot's ass.

"Wow, this place is a shithole!" cried a horrified Ansell.

Embarrassed, Andrew didn't know what to say.

"You can't bring a woman here; you don't even have a proper bed. Fucking hell!"

Andrew wondered if it had occurred to this brute that he hadn't even been invited.

"Look, it's really nice of you to pop by, but I'm a bit tired at the moment. I just need some quiet time to myself."

"Hey bruv, that's cool. You might want to change that music though, it's not exactly soothing."

Andrew thought that if this plonker called him 'Bruv' one more time, he might just risk life and limb to smash him on the nose.

"Another time, okay?" said Ansell, going to the door.

"Yeah." Andrew slammed the door behind him.

'Only if hell freezes over,' he thought to himself.

Sunday, 9 a.m.

Andrew didn't sleep well. He should have been grateful that he'd had a whole week of work and that he had another one lined up. Walking back and forth to Liverpool Street was painful, but at least he was working. However, with Ansell discovering that he had a crush on the waitress and the fact that he had described his flat as a "Shithole," Andrew realised he had a long way to go. No matter how many times he thought things were getting better, there was always something that would remind him they weren't. He was still working in a shitty job, living in a shitty flat, and still had no friends and no prospects. Andrew felt that familiar feeling of despair as it began to cover him like a blanket. He lay in bed, really not wanting to leave it. However, he knew he had to force himself to do something. He could have put a lot of time into cleaning his flat but it felt too oppressive to him, so he decided the best thing to do was go out.

Money was the ongoing problem. He faced another week of walking back and forth to work and yet he still found himself purchasing a cheap newspaper and heading to the café. Beatrice was already there, rummaging through her numerous bags; the professor was watching her, perturbed. It was very busy as the usual Sunday punters, still wearing the same clothes from the previous night, gathered and had their normal fry-ups. There was a lot of friendly banter. As soon as Andrew sat down, the waitress approached him, smiling.

"Can I have an egg and bacon meal and a cappuccino please?"

"Sure," replied the waitress. "Is your friend okay now?"

"He's not my friend," snapped Andrew, instantly regretting it.

"That's a shame," she replied calmly. "He seemed like a nice man and would make a great friend."

That confirmed it. Ansell was just the type of black man she would like; heavily-muscled, with that 'grinning idiot' vibe.

"I don't know about that, he's just someone from around the area. He took me by surprise yesterday."

"I understand. I'll get your order."

Andrew made a show of looking at his newspaper. Whatever remote chance he'd had of ever going out with this waitress, it had gone forever. He couldn't concentrate on the paper and when he received his order, he quickly ate it and then walked out of the café, almost bumping into Cliff as he entered. Cliff grunted angrily but Andrew hardly noticed or cared.

Approaching his flat, he noticed a small minivan was parked in front of it. As he neared his gate, Ansell popped out, causing Andrew to jump.

"What's up, bro?"

"Nothing," replied Andrew. *'Dear God,'* he thought, *'make him go away.'*

"Good, I've got a spare stove that's been knocking about my house for a while. It's in good condition, so I thought I'd sort you out."

"What?!" exclaimed Andrew.

"Don't worry mate, I know the landlord and I've got all the necessary bits sorted out. I've done so many jobs for him and this is listed under 'essential improvements. Stop staring and open the door."

135

Andrew was not much of a DIY person. He found the whole DIY craze a little bit insane and considered himself far too intellectual to do that kind of work. However, he had to admit he admired Ansell's passion for his work. As Andrew handed Ansell the tools he needed, he found himself respecting the change in him. Gone was the happy-go-lucky guy; Ansell now seemed a serious person that was dedicated to doing a very professional job.

It was just after two in the afternoon when Ansell finished the job. Andrew now found himself looking at a stove in the hallway, which meant when he cooked, he wouldn't have to have the smell of food drifting into the living room as much. Commenting on how hungry he was, Ansell insisted on treating them to lunch at a local burger restaurant on Portobello Road.

Sunday, 2:30 p.m.

At lunch, Ansell talked a lot about where he came from. He was a self-employed builder that had built up his business over the years, to where he could now afford the finer things in life. He bought a three-bedroom house in Shepherd's Bush years ago and now had enough money to only take the work that suited him. He simply loved the work he did. His main aim was to make sure his two daughters were set up for life.

Ansell was this force of nature that seemed to enjoy life. Although he was upset at being dumped by Shannon, once he had got drunk and grieved over the situation, he felt that the next day was a new one and it was time to move on and explore all that life had to offer. Andrew wished he could bounce back quickly from adversity. Instead, he seemed to constantly dwell on setbacks and never seemed to get over life's knocks.

Sitting in the restaurant, feeling pleasantly full, Ansell looked at the menu.

"Fancy a desert, mate?"

"No, thanks," replied Andrew, "I don't think I can eat another drop."

"How about a coffee?"

"That's not a bad idea," replied Andrew, feeling embarrassed that not only had Ansell provided him with a stove, but he had also bought lunch. Andrew promised himself that one day he would somehow return the favour, although he didn't know when, considering he still had to walk to work for the whole of the week.

"Hi love, can we have two cappuccinos?" said Ansell. Then to Andrew, he said, "I noticed you had a lot of painting materials hanging about. Are you an artist?"

"I use to think of myself as one. I studied art in uni."

"Yeah? That's wicked man, do you still paint?"

"No man, you can't make a living doing that."

"What are you, mad? With social media, you can do so many things. I know a man making nuff dollars doing art, man. Fuck, I went to an exhibition where a bloke put a dirty pair of trainers on a canvas and called that art! I don't remember how much they sold it for but it was advertised for £1000. Why can't you stick a pair of old shoes on a canvas and see how much you can get for that? I'm sure I've got an old pair of smelly shoes hanging about that I can give you, I wouldn't even take a cut."

Andrew smiled, "I don't think it works like that."

"I dunno, man. It seems to me that a lot of so-called artists get away with murder, man. That Tracy Emin, as much as I'd like to shag her, puts out bare rubbish and gets paid. And what about that Banksy bloke? I don't remember seeing anything by him that I like. It's a smoke-and-mirrors business. You must have painted or done something outrageous like that."

Andrew suddenly remembered:

"Well, once I painted a skull and crossbones for a laugh. Instead of a skull, I painted a vagina and instead of bones, I painted penises."

"No way!" laughed Ansell. "That's the type of rubbish that people like! I don't mean it that way, but, well, you know what I mean. What did you do with it?"

138

"I gave it to someone I knew from uni. His father ran a restaurant for years. This bloke thought that if he had a few pieces of art on display, then it would give the restaurant a more upmarket image. He promised me that if he could sell it, he would give me the money, minus ten percent commission. I thought he was full of it so that's why I made that painting. It was supposed to be a joke, but the funny thing was, the bloke loved it and said he would put it up right away."

"Did it sell?"

"I don't know actually," replied Andrew. "I never did follow it up. I just thought the guy was a bit of an idiot for wanting it in the first place."

"Man, I would check out what happened to it if I were you. For all you know, you could be the next Banksy." Ansell made a puking gesture with his hands.

"Maybe I should," replied Andrew.

"You should. This art thing sounds mad and if you got talent, you should go for it. Working in a mailroom somehow doesn't suit you."

"It's a living," replied Andrew.

Ansell's stare of concern took Andrew by surprise.

"Wow, fancy meeting you here, old chap."

Andrew recognised that voice and his guess was confirmed when he saw the swaggering figure of Edward approaching them. Charlotte was holding his hand. Edward wore a black hoodie with jeans, while Charlotte was wearing a mini-skirt and a simple black top. Edward put his fist out, which Andrew reluctantly touched; Ansell was a lot more enthusiastic. Charlotte kissed both men on the cheeks. Andrew noted the smell of expensive perfume.

"Well Ansell, I didn't know you knew Andrew," spoke Edward.

"He's my mate," replied Ansell.

"I'm so sorry to hear about you and Shannon," put in Charlotte. "How are you holding up?"

"Don't worry about me, I'm blessed."

"Good to know," replied Edward. "Well, it looks like our food is here. We fancied a takeaway. See you later."

Ansell caught Andrew discreetly watching Charlotte's legs as they grabbed their food and walked out of the restaurant.

"I know, I know," commented Ansell.

Andrew was embarrassed.

"I wish I had a relationship like them, they really seem to love each other," said Ansell.

"I could do with them loving each other a little less," replied Andrew.

"Don't be like that, bruv."

'Here he goes with that "bruv" stuff again,' thought Andrew.

"I mean it," commented Andrew. "And what's that all about, doing it after EastEnders?"

"What?"

"They always have sex after EastEnders!"

"Really?" laughed Ansell. "How do you know it's after "EastEnders?"

"Because they turn the bloody TV on too loud, that's how. My floorboards are so thin, I can hear Edward, as you'd say, 'beating it up'," replied Andrew, finding himself starting to smile.

140

"No way!" replied Ansell, with that big booming laugh of his. "You can actually hear them tearing it up?"

"Every ting," Andrew surprised himself by speaking in patois.

Ansell shook his head.

"I'm suffering man, I really am suffering. Just imagine this; first, you hear the sound of tom, tom, tom…" Andrew imitated the famous closing bars of EastEnders. "Followed by, 'come on baby, come on. I'm coming baby, I'm coming. Go on baby, do it, do it'. Followed by 'Ah, ah, argggh!' That's what I've got to put up with," replied Andrew, realising that Donna's dramatic way of expressing herself seemed to have rubbed off on him.

"Really?" laughed Ansell.

"Bloody annoying. And another thing, what's with Edward always thinking like he has to act black around me? He's a fucking prick!"

"That's a bit harsh, mate. We were born here but we don't always speak patois in front of white people. Instead, we speak in a way we think they will understand; in a way that will make them feel more comfortable."

"It's different mate, and you know it," spoke Andrew. "If we spoke patois all the time, we wouldn't get work. I can't rock up to a job interview and start saying, 'De man dem this,' or 'De man dem that' and expect to get the job. If an interviewer asks me how am I doing today, I don't say 'Irie, I'm blessed,' do I? So in a sense, we have to conform because if we don't integrate with society, we won't survive. But Edward does not have that issue. He *is* society. A lot of his dosh is from inherited wealth, for all we know, it could have come from his ancestors exploiting brown people from somewhere in the world. Maybe acting black is his way of making up for that. I don't know and I don't care. What I do know is that throughout his whole life, he will never have experienced some of the things I've experienced trying to get work or just trying to make sense of things. So why can't he just be what he is and stop feeling the need to pretend to be black? He's an asshole."

Ansell shook his head, suddenly changing the subject.

"What about that girl, when are you going to ask her out?"

"Not going to happen," replied Andrew.

"Why man? She's fit."

"Let's not go there," replied Andrew.

"Don't take this the wrong way," replied Ansell, "but you're a bit uptight. Maybe a good seeing to is what you need."

"Look, mate, you know how guys like to talk about women in a certain way? I'm not that guy. I don't go around with a bunch of blokes saying how this girl is fit or how she's got a great ass. It's not me. If a girl is nice, I'll notice, but I don't go around saying what I'd like to do with her," said Andrew.

"Maybe you should, bro," replied Ansell. "It's a great way to get things off your chest and it's a nice little banter between blokes."

"Maybe," replied Andrew. "But my mother didn't raise me that way."

"Really bro?" replied Ansell. "Let me ask you, when was the last time you was in a serious relationship?"

"Err, three years ago."

"No way!" replied Ansell, a look of shock on his face. Andrew could not hide the look of hurt as he suddenly thought about Kadisa.

The Breakup

Walking out of the building, Andrew hoped that the fresh air would clear his head a bit. He was never a social drinker at the best of times and having a glass of champagne before lunch was not something that he had expected to do. Andrew found himself feeling slightly tipsy for most of the day and he struggled to do his job with his usual efficiently. Nobody minded as the whole company seemed to be on a 'go-slow day' that day.

Earlier that day, Andrew had been on his first mail run when there was an announcement over the intercom broadcasting the fact that the company had just won a major contract. It congratulated everyone on all the hard work they'd put in to achieve it.

When Andrew arrived back at the mailroom, Peter, John, Donna, Andi, Marcia and the chairman of the company were all standing together, holding champagne glasses. Andrew recognised the Chairman from pictures: he was a plump man in his forties, shorter than he had imagined, with an engaging smile. Peter had gestured to Andrew to pick up a glass and then popped open the champagne. The champagne had gone straight to Andrew's head; he could hardly pay attention to Marcia as she mentioned that every staff member was to receive a bonus and that she had spoken to the chairman, who had agreed that Andrew was to get a little extra in his salary as well.

The day went by in a haze for Andrew. Standing outside the company building, he mentally prepared himself for the long walk home.

Andrew was grateful for the two weeks of work. If they kept their promise of giving him the bonus, that would be great. However, even without the bonus, the fact that he had been working consistently meant that the following week he would now be able to afford the bus or train to work. Andrew thought it ironic that now he had the money for travel fares, he didn't have any work for the upcoming week; it was just the type of scenario he was used to.

Walking the familiar route home, Andrew wondered if he should start to call agencies to let them know he was available for work the following week. He still had a few days to go and a lot could happen in that time, but having experienced times when he'd had a spurt of work and then everything dried up again, he didn't want to rest on his laurels. He knew that with his phone credit running low, he couldn't make as many calls as he would like until Friday, when he would be able to top it up. However, Peter was quite good in the way that once the work was finished, he didn't mind him using the internet to do whatever he wanted.

Andrew would miss working for Kane Publishing; it was a great company to work for, even in the mailroom. The way the company looked after their staff was incredible, and there was a real family atmosphere that Andrew had never experienced anywhere else. Since working for Kane, he had even felt less sorry for himself. However, he now had to be realistic; there was more chance of him finding work in a company that was dull and exploitative than one that was as progressive as Kane Publishing. Gloom set in.

The lunch he'd had the previous Sunday had proved interesting. He had found Ansell's reaction to him being single for over three years a bit disturbing. It was as if Ansell couldn't understand how an experience could hurt so much that you didn't want to be hurt that way ever again. The concept seemed to fly right over his head. Ansell was the type of person that Andrew couldn't understand at all. He goes out with woman number one; the relationship doesn't work out but they now have a daughter. The daughter now lives with the mother and from time to time, sees Ansell. Ansell then goes out with woman number two; she also becomes pregnant and they end up with the same arrangement. Even after all that drama, Ansell seemed to continuously go through life sleeping with women, never learning from his mistakes. It probably didn't occur to him to stop thinking only with his genitals. What kind of person was he? What puzzled Andrew even more, was what kind of woman would date someone like Ansell, knowing the type of track record he had. Did they imagine that the outcome with them would be different? To Andrew, who thought women wanted a guy to have his act together—a decent job, no skeletons in the closet—the whole scenario was confusing.

Andrew's experience had been a painful one and one that he wanted to learn from. He struggled to come to terms with the fact that Kadisa did not want to be with him anymore. It felt as if her personality had changed so much, Andrew no longer recognised the woman that stood in front of him. Everything felt like it was out of the blue for Andrew; looking back, perhaps he should have read the signs.

It was strange that they were together in the first place. Kadisa was very popular in university. She loved to party and although she studied, it was never

146

her priority. Andrew, on the other hand, was studious and worked part-time to fund his studies. Whereas she had many friends, James was Andrew's only friend. He simply didn't have the time to socialise, and he was determined that all the sacrifices his mother had made were not going to be in vain. Kadisa was not the type of girl Andrew thought would be interested in him, not that he knew what type would be, and when they got together, his mother thought the same. She never liked Kadisa and was not shy in saying so. They had started talking on the day they were put together to work on a class project and Kadisa was fascinated by the fact that Andrew had savings and had a financial plan. Most of the other guys lived for today and if they had anything like a car, it was usually gained through their parents or illegal activities. Yet despite their differences, they became a couple.

They would spend the weekends together after Andrew finished work, and during the week, they would meet up in school. Andrew was serious about his studies, nothing was going to get in the way of that, and this irritated her at times. Other than that, they were very happy and spent their time talking about their dreams for the future: Andrew would be the famous artist and she would be the CEO of a multinational company.

After graduating from university, Kadisa had found a job almost immediately, as a trainee manager at one of the more prestigious fashion houses. She did have a keen interest in fashion and given her grades, which were average at best, she was grateful for the job. In the initial stages, she had found herself struggling with the demands of the job until one of the directors took her under his wing and helped her to get to grips with her new role. They started to hang out together and he introduced her to a whole new circle of friends. At the same time, Andrew had quickly found a job in arts administration and also found the flat, which wasn't the best but it didn't matter; it was the start of bigger things. Andrew planned to work hard at the company, make connections, and gradually start promoting his art. They were on their way to getting married and having a life together.

The last time they made love, it had been the best sex of Andrew's life. Kadisa was attractive and loved sex, but somehow, Andrew didn't see her as sexy. In the back of Andrew's mind, there had always been something about her that disturbed him. He never acknowledged it at the time, but he was constantly on guard and could never really relax intimately. However, the last time they had made love, it had felt different in every way. She was different. She smelled different. Everything felt strange and wonderful. It was supposed to be the night they christened the flat; once they had saved up, they would get a better place and move in together.

The next day, instead of staying in bed together, Kadisa insisted they go to a local café and have breakfast. It was then she dropped the bombshell that their relationship was over. Andrew pleaded with her to give the relationship a chance as they had been together all through university, but she insisted. She had moved on and now lived in a whole new world; Andrew simply wasn't part of it.

Andrew had tried to stay away but found that he couldn't. Surely all he needed to do was to meet with Kadisa and try to make her see sense? In the past, they'd had a few arguments but had always made up again. Surely this was the same situation. He tried calling her several times but her phone always seemed to go to voicemail. This was not happening, it all seemed to be so unreal; there had to be a way to resolve this. Then, in a fit of desperation, Andrew found himself rushing over to Kadisa's flat. When her roommate had opened the door and told him that it was not a good time as Kadisa was sleeping, he should have listened. But instead, Andrew pushed past her roommate and barged into her bedroom, only to see Kadisa's nude body straggling on top of another man.

Andrew struggled for breath and then spontaneously threw up. The man covered himself up, looking surprised and embarrassed. Although Kadisa was shouting at him, Andrew found it difficult to make out what she was saying. Her mouth was moving, but she seemed so far away, and Andrew felt a throbbing pain in his head. Then suddenly, he could understand her—she was calling him an idiot and telling him to get out.

Andrew never remembered the journey back to his flat; he just somehow made it back and never left his bed for a week. His whole world had collapsed. How could someone sleep with someone, knowing that the next day they were planning to dump them? How could anyone be so cruel? The only thing that Andrew could think of was that she hadn't loved him in the first place; that perhaps she had been lying all that time. In that case, why would someone do that to another human being and why had he been stupid enough not to see the signs?

Andrew was so engrossed in his thoughts that he didn't register that someone had said something to him. He turned around to see the waitress from the café smiling at him. She wore the same outfit that she'd worn the other week. Andrew quickly wiped away the tears that had formed in his eyes.

Anna

"I thought I recognised you," smiled the waitress, extending her hand for Andrew to shake. Andrew gingerly shook her hand, embarrassed by the fact that his palms were sweaty. "How are you?"

"I'm good," replied Andrew.

"Finished work?"

"Yeah, I'm meeting up with friends. What you are up to?"

"I'm going to dance class."

"Dance class, really?"

"Yes, I'm a dancer. I study at Ballet Rambert and I also take classes at Pineapple Dance Studios."

"Wow, that sounds great."

"It's nothing really, dancing is what I've always wanted to do. What about you?"

"I'm temping at a publishing company, but I am really a visual artist."

"Really? I'd love to see your work."

"Thanks, perhaps I'll bring some into the café sometime," Andrew said, realising that he hadn't painted or drawn anything for a long time, other than the sketch of her, and he wasn't sure if she'd think that was a bit strange.

"That would be really nice," replied the waitress. "I've always admired artists, I'm hopeless at painting."

"We have something in common," replied Andrew. "I can't dance to save my life—even my two left feet have two left feet."

The waitress laughed. Making her laugh felt like sunshine washing over him. He wanted this moment to last forever.

"That sounds like a deal. Anyway, I am so sorry, I've got to rush as I'm running late. Nice talking to you, err…"

"Andrew, my name's Andrew."

"I'm Anna. See you on Saturday?"

"Yes, see you then."

Andrew watched as Anna walked down the street. The walk home was the most pleasant he'd had all week.

Saturday, 6:30 a.m.

There was something about Hyde Park in the morning that Andrew loved; the smell of freshly cut grass, the sound of birds chirping away, and only a few joggers around. It was beautiful. Andrew jogged past Princess Diana's Memorial Park thinking that, in a few hours, it would be filled with excitable children. The weather forecast predicted that it would be a glorious day.

Andrew was still upbeat about his conversation with Anna. Anna—what a beautiful name. Andrew and Anna Smalls; it definitely had a certain ring to it. The rest of the week seemed to fly by, with Andrew actually enjoying his work and looking forward to seeing Anna again. On Friday, it had been his last day working in the mailroom and the guys were very nice, bringing in champagne as a thank you for his good work. The girls came to see him too, bringing the usual dish of chicken, rice and peas. Andrew didn't have any work coming up the following week, but his mood was so upbeat that he didn't even bother to make any calls.

Meeting Anna and knowing that she was a dancer had made Andrew think about his fitness. His diet in recent months for the most part had been awful and he hardly did any exercise. He decided he should do something about it.

Andrew had never really been the sporty type, choosing instead to spend all his spare time drawing. So he had been surprised when, in secondary school, he was chosen to be in the school football team. He hadn't been particularly skilled, but he'd had a knack of reading the game extremely well. It surprised him that his analytical skills could be useful in football; he had a knack of knowing exactly where he needed to be to make the maximum effect without expending an excessive amount of energy. So he was often stuck in midfield, where his love of tackling and his excellent ability to time his tackle was put to good use. He had been quite happy to sit in midfield, plug the holes, and once he won the ball, pass it to the more skilful players.

Andrew was now determined to be in a better physical condition; he started by trying to do things at home. Perhaps he could do sit-ups, push-ups, or even jogging on the spot? However, by the time he got home and prepared something to eat, he was too tired. So he decided that it would be better to do something at the weekend.

Andrew woke up at six in the morning, picked out a pair of jogging pants along with a t-shirt, a bottle of water and set out on his way. He figured if he ran around Hyde Park once, he would be in time to have a shower and get to the café to see Anna.

Andrew surprised himself by jogging all the way up to Portobello Road, then to the top of Notting Hill, without a problem. He even found himself enjoying the physicality of it all. As long as he could manage to pace himself, he would be fine. Andrew took a swig of water and entered the park.

After jogging along for another five minutes, Andrew suddenly saw Edward and Charlotte heading towards him, joined by an extremely well-built Latin man who was around Andrew's age. He wore plain jogging pants and a vest. He had tattooed arms and carried himself with the arrogance of someone who knew he was God's gift to women.

"Well, Hello Andrew. Doing a spot of jogging?!" exclaimed Edward, making a show of lifting his knees higher as he and Charlotte jogged on the spot.

'No, I'm ten pin bowling, you idiot,' Andrew wanted to say. Instead, he found himself saying, "I just thought I'd go for a quick run around the park."

"Be careful, dear boy. I don't think you have that type of stamina. Perhaps you should have started by jogging around the block, just to get your body used to running."

"I'll be okay," said Andrew, as he thought, *'Fucking prick'.*

"It is good that you're working on your fitness," said Charlotte. "Perhaps if you can afford it, you can have a personal trainer, like we do. This is Javier."

"Hello," Javier shook Andrew's hand and without Edward noticing, grabbed Charlotte's bottom at the same time. It was such a split-second move that Andrew wondered if it was an accident. Either way, Charlotte didn't seem to mind. "Nice to meet you."

"Likewise," replied Andrew, trying to process what he had just seen.

"Come on dear, let's do another lap," said Edward. "See you later, young man."

"Bye," replied Andrew, glad to be running in the opposite direction.

Five minutes later, Andrew was jogging when a dog appeared out of nowhere. It rushed up to him and proceeded to bark angrily.

"Fucking hell!" screamed Andrew, frightened. "Get away from me."

The owner, an apologetic young man, rushed up to the dog and pulled him away.

"They invented a lead for a reason, you fucking moron!"

Angrily, Andrew sprinted away at full pelt. He was never completely at ease with dogs and never understood people who petted ones that didn't belong to them. His mother once said to him that when she was growing up in Jamaica, dogs were not allowed in their house. Also, on the rare occasions they visited friends that had a dog, they would never accept food from them unless they saw them properly wash their hands. As far as Andrew was concerned, most dogs were simply one bark away from attacking him. If a dog didn't just approach him calmly, his pulse rate would dramatically increase. Andrew particularly hated the people who proudly walked down the street with fierce-looking dogs, often without them on leads. He had a theory that they had these dogs as some sort of compensation for having a small penis.

Andrew's sprint eventually slowed to a gentle jog and he was just starting to enjoy the scenery again when he suddenly felt a sharp pain in his left calf. It gripped it like a vice and shot up the back of his thigh; the pain was so intense that he collapsed to the ground in agony, letting out a loud scream. It was cramp. He tried to be calm and relax in order to ride out the pain. He even tried slow breathing. However, the pain was excruciating. Lying on the grass, Andrew realised that going for a run was the worst thing he could have done. After spending the whole week walking back and forth to work, there was no way he was in any condition to jog. It was then he realised that having a crush on someone was definitely not good for your health.

As he lay on the floor, Andrew noticed Edward, Charlotte and Javier jogging cheerfully towards him. Quickly, he panicked. How did they get around the park so fast? Had they just doubled back? These were obviously the last people he wanted to see, especially as he was in too much pain and too tired to stand. Thankfully, they were so engrossed in conversation, they didn't notice Andrew. Looking around frantically, he spotted a small bush a good five yards away. With every ounce of strength he had, he dragged himself across the grass, pulling his body forward. His arms ached, the sticks and stones dug into his body, and his leg was still seized up with the sharp pain from the cramp, but there was no way Andrew was going to let Edward see him this way; his pride simply wouldn't allow it. Andrew frantically pulled himself until he was behind the bush. Knowing that he was safely hidden, he lay there, panting for breath, and watched as Edward, Charlotte, and their personal trainer jogged by.

Andrew lay on the grass for a while. He was totally exhausted and his tracksuit was covered in dirt and grass. He massaged his calf and waited until the pain eventually subsided. Andrew was not in the mood to continue and decided that he'd better make his way home. He was very disappointed with himself for not completing his run. However, at this point, all he wanted to do was have a hot shower and go to sleep. Andrew looked around; he was around the Knightsbridge area and having brought no money with him, it was going to be a long walk home. It was a painful process, with Andrew stopping and resting frequently. By the time he got back to the flat, it was already lunchtime. Depressed over missing breakfast at the café and not seeing

Anna, Andrew felt that familiar feeling of despair. As all hope drained from his body, taking his strength with it, Andrew drank some water and fell asleep.

Around 6 p.m., Andrew was awoken by the sound of the bell ringing. He peered discreetly out the window and saw Ansell cheerfully standing outside. Andrew was not in the mood and went back to sleep, ignoring the ringing of his mobile phone.

Sunday, 9:15 a.m.

Andrew sleepily looked at his phone. It was the second time in so many days that he had woken up this late but he felt as if he had hardly slept. Every part of Andrew's body was in pain. Perhaps if he lay in bed and tried some relaxation exercises, he would feel better. Then he remembered Anna. He didn't see her yesterday and he didn't want to miss seeing her today.

Jumping out of bed, Andrew rushed to the bathroom, washed his face and threw on some clothes. Walking out the door, he felt the familiar sense of despair take over him. He was rushing over to a café to see a woman that would probably never see him as someone she would date, she was just being friendly. Why was he torturing himself? After a few weeks of constant work, Andrew was grateful that he could now afford public transport to travel to work, but the truth was, he had no work for the following week. Surely the smart thing to do was to save money. He needed to start making calls again; experience told him that he could end up not getting work for a while. He needed to spend Sunday planning his week; he shouldn't be letting emotion get in the way of logic or else he could end up like James.

Guilt overwhelmed him for not visiting his friend. From time-to-time, he would see him chatting happily to his friend Mike or begging for money at his spot. James and his new-found friend formed a bit of a double act standing outside Ladbroke Grove, asking for money. Andrew avoided him whenever he could, as he didn't have the strength to deal with James. It was bad enough that he was letting his emotions get carried away with Anna; he couldn't face having to solve James' issues too.

Andrew stood in front of the café, reasoning that popping in was okay, as long as he spent the rest of the day productively.

As usual, the café was busy: the professor was pacing up and down; Cliff was quiet for once, eating breakfast; Anna smiled at Andrew as he found a seat. Andrew felt a wave of joy that he could never have imagined in the past.

"Egg and Bacon?" she asked, rushing past him.

Andrew nodded with a smile. He tried not to stare at her as she walked up to the counter. Andrew opened his newspaper, scanned the pages, and found the news was depressing as usual. He quickly moved to the sports pages.

A moment later, Anna walked up to his table, placed his coffee down and to his surprise, sat down opposite him.

"Morning Andrew, how are you?"

"I'm good at the moment. How are you?"

"I'm very well. Did you enjoy your night out with friends?"

Andrew struggled to remember and then blurted out, "Oh, it got cancelled; a few people couldn't make it." Andrew surprised himself with how easily he could lie.

"Oh, that must have been disappointing."

"That's how it is sometimes. How was your class?

"It was okay, but I have so much to do. I am working on a short piece based on the suffragette movement; I also have English homework and a paper to do."

"Sounds like you have a lot on your plate," said Andrew, not knowing what to say.

"On your plate?" asked Anna, confused.

"Oh, that just means that you're very busy."

"Yes, I am," replied Anna. "I'm not sure how I will be able to fit them all in, it's so overwhelming."

"One step at a time," replied Andrew. "That's all you have to do. Break the tasks into smaller steps and then put all your energy into accomplishing the small tasks. You can do it; I believe you can."

"That's very nice of you to say."

"Sure, worry wastes so much energy, just focus on what you can do." Andrew couldn't believe he was saying this. Love was making him into a bit of a tosser and he was puzzled as to why he couldn't listen to his own advice.

"Very smart, Andrew, I think I will try that," replied Anna, seemingly grateful to let that out. "So, where is the art you were going to show me?"

"Er, to be honest, I haven't had much time to do any drawing at the moment."

"You could show me anything, it doesn't have to be new."

"It's just that I'm like you, I have to make a living, and my art wasn't really paying."

"It's your passion. You should be doing something about it, no matter what," replied Anna.

"Maybe," replied Andrew, realising that Ansell had been saying the same thing. Perhaps he should try to find out what happened to his skull and crossbones painting.

"It's not a maybe—just do it. I'd really like to see your work."

Andrew wondered what she would think of the sketch he'd done of her recently. She'd probably think he was a bit too weird.

The professor walked past them, picked up a cigarette, and went outside to smoke. Cliff shook his head.

"Less than two hours to go," commented Cliff.

"I know," replied Anna.

Seeing Andrew's confused face, Anna explained:

"When the professor comes here in the morning, he puts a napkin on the table, followed by a glass, and then he opens his thermos and pours himself some tea. At twelve o'clock, he takes out his bottle of red wine, drains the remainder of his tea, and pours the wine in."

"That's right!" exclaimed Cliff. "Then, around two o'clock, he leaves the café, takes the 70 bus—and it has to be the 70 bus because it stops just in front of where Whiteley's used to be—goes to a local café in the area, puts the napkin on the table, and pours himself a glass of wine. Then he stays there for hours."

"Really!" exclaimed Andrew, suddenly whispering. "How do you know?"

"I saw him, that's how," Cliff replied. "Young people nowadays."

"Don't be too hard on him," replied Anna, winking at Andrew. "He doesn't have the benefit of your age and pearls of wisdom."

"That's quite correct," put in Cliff in a huff. "I blame all that time they spend on social media, it dulls the senses. Anyway, speaking of Pearl, how is our lady?"

"She said yes."

"You're kidding me?" replied Cliff, astonished.

"It's not a joke, she's getting married."

Andrew couldn't believe it.

"It's not to the same bloke who caused a scene the other day, is it?" he asked.

"It is," replied Anna. "It's so romantic; reminds me of that old film, *An Officer and A Gentleman.*"

"Oh yeah, I remember that movie, Lou Gossett Jr was good in that," said Cliff.

'There's something about that bloody movie,' thought Andrew, remembering his fantasies about saving Anna.

Anna cast her eyes on Alfie, who was looking on disapprovingly.

"It looks like the boss, wants you," put in Cliff.

"I'd better get to the other customers."

The flow of customers kept coming in. Anna managed to give Andrew his breakfast and he watched as she worked hard at serving the others. She was a brilliant waitress. Gladys still worked during the weekdays, so she must have had to come in very early to change the place around before starting work.

After a while, Andrew got up to leave. As he walked out the door, Anna called out: "Have a good day!"

"Thanks, you too," replied Andrew.

Andrew left the café feeling as if he could skip down the road. If only it didn't hurt so much.

Are You Andrew Smalls?

Andrew's lungs were bursting, he could still feel the after-effects of the cramp, and his legs were in terrible pain. He didn't know how long he could keep going, but he had to, he had to run. He turned around the corner, but they were still chasing him. Andrew's only hope of escape was to run into the park; surely they wouldn't be able to find him there? Whatever momentary relief he felt upon entering the park was gone, when Andrew realised that no matter how hard he ran, the scenery didn't change—the trees, the grass and the Princess Di memorial were ever-present. He couldn't seem to get away from them.

The sounds of a dog barking in the distance seemed to be getting closer and closer. He had to get away. Andrew tried pushing himself harder, but he struggled for breath and his heart was pounding so hard that he was afraid of having a heart attack. The dog had almost caught up with him and in that second, it made a gigantic leap, grabbing Andrew's trouser leg and ripping it. Andrew staggered, worried that his only decent work trousers were ruined. Where would he get the money to purchase new ones? The dog lunged at Andrew again; a sharp pain in his ankle caused him to collapse in a heap. He couldn't move anymore, and he waited for death to come. The dog sensed victory and its features started to change into something that resembled a smile. Joining the dog were Pearl, Cliff, Bea and Alfie, all dressed in 1920s gangster-style suits. Each one of them held a placard with the words 'Rent', 'Telephone', 'Electricity', and 'Council Tax' written on them. The professor joined the group, holding a suitcase with the word 'Bailiff' written on it. Behind him, two policemen followed. Andrew could hear his name being repeatedly called out on a radio.

"Andrew Smalls, we are arresting you for non-payment of bills. Andrew Smalls, Andrew smalls, is this the right place?"

Andrew jumped from his bed, sweating heavily. He looked around and found he was at home; it was a dream. He could hear the bell ringing and a mobile phone buzzing.

He could hear a voice outside.

"It is Andrew Smalls, isn't it?

Andrew's pulse was racing. Should he answer the door? He looked out the window and saw a bike messenger standing in front of his door; he appeared to be talking to someone on his mobile phone. Andrew had a sudden fear that perhaps he was going to get a hand-delivered letter summoning him to court. Andrew heard the voice again.

"I'm not sure if the phone's working. I'll give it one more try."

Andrew wasn't sure what to think, but he decided he'd better face the music, whatever it was. Taking a deep breath, Andrew opened the door.

"Are you Andrew Smalls?"

"Yes?"

"Can you call Agnes, ASAP?"

"Okay," replied a confused Andrew, shutting the door.

Checking his mobile phone, there were several missed calls on it. His phone was on silent and he had overslept. It was 9.30 a.m.

Andrew dialled the number.

"Agnes, its Andrew."

"Andrew, thank goodness, I've been trying to reach you. Kane Publishing wants you back doing your original work. What time can you get there?

Andrew couldn't believe that an employment agency would send a bike messenger out to alert him about work. That had never happened to him before and he couldn't imagine it was something that would ever happen again. Agnes was amazing. Andrew remembered that although he didn't have to walk to work anymore, he would still need time to sort out work clothes.

"Probably in an hour and a half."

"Good," replied Agnes. "I'll let them know. By the way, it's for six months, are you okay with that?"

"Fantastic!" exclaimed Andrew.

"Good, get yourself sorted and I'll talk to you later."

Andrew said goodbye to Agnes and then collapsed to the floor in tears.

Saturday, 7:40 a.m.

It was a bit chilly for the time of year, but then again, English weather was always unpredictable. Andrew made a point of putting on his jacket, along with a scarf and hat. The last thing Andrew wanted was to fall ill. Walking out of his flat, Andrew noticed two bodybuilders walking down the street wearing vests. Andrew wondered if having muscles was some sort of insulation against the cold. They were the type of guys Andrew hated, mainly due to the way they looked at everyone that wasn't built like them. They viewed you like you were the scum of the earth.

On his way to Tesco, Andrew reflected on what had essentially been a really good week for him. It was great to be with Donna and Andi again. Donna had broken up with her boyfriend after apparently finding out that whilst seeing her, he had fathered a two-year-old daughter with another woman. She only found out when the woman called at her house looking for her partner because he had missed his child support payments. Donna told the story, showing the frustration and deep hurt she felt over what had happened. However, Andrew also felt that she enjoyed being the centre of attention. Cruelly, Andrew noted to himself, that despite being a 'footer', he would not have done that to anyone he was seeing.

Andi's situation was also different. She was lucky enough to have landed herself a leading role in a fringe theatre production but she was finding it increasingly difficult to juggle two jobs and would often be seen yawning. At lunchtime, she would simply curl up on the sofa and fall asleep.

Andrew now felt confident to open up to them about Anna. Both girls were wondering why he didn't just ask her out, when it wouldn't be the end of the world if she said no.

'Speak for yourself,' Andrew thought.

Andi told him that he should not underestimate himself, while Donna volunteered to coach him on how to ask her out. Andrew politely declined, reasoning that with her background in relationships, she was the last person he would seek advice from.

Andrew felt it was extremely important that he was worthy of having someone like Anna and in that regard, he felt she would be more impressed if he actually was an artist. So he took out his sketch pads and started thinking about the type of things he'd like to draw. He found it strange to think about art again and to his surprise, he was excited at the idea of exploring the world through pencil and paper once more.

He then tried to find out what exactly had happened to his skull and crossbones painting. He vaguely remembered that the guy who had taken it was called Jeff, but he didn't know his surname, so he went about researching the name and address of his father's restaurant. When he made the call, he found that Jeff was very glad to hear from him, as they had been trying to track him down for months. Jeff told him that he had sold it for five-hundred pounds and wondered whether he could do some more. "The weirder, the better," according to him. Jeff explained that initially, his father thought it was a bad idea to put the painting up in the restaurant, reasoning that it would put off clients, so it stayed in storage. It probably would have stayed there indefinitely if the business had been going well. However, business took a turn for the worse, mainly because it was too similar to the other restaurants in the area—good food, very slick, but unfortunately bland. Jeff took a chance and started a major rebranding exercise—he hung the painting up, sold all the furniture, brought some second sofas, simplified the menu, added some jazz and blues background music, and right away, business picked up. They started to attract artists from all walks of life and within weeks the painting had created a big buzz. Shortly after that, it was sold. After speaking to Andrew for a while, he put Andrew through to the accounts department and they took his bank details. Moments later, he was five-hundred pounds richer. Andrew couldn't believe it. They didn't even want commission because the painting had drawn such a following of art enthusiasts and bohemian types, that business was booming. Andrew had called at exactly the right time because Jeff could now look forward to promising more great work from *"The Mystery Artist."*

Armed with the extra five-hundred pounds, Andrew was still too afraid to hope that things were actually getting better. So, even with a steady job and a little bit of extra money, he wasn't going to rest on his laurels. During his lunchtime, Andrew would make a flurry of phone calls in the hope of picking up the occasional bit of bar work in the evenings. With a lot of positive responses, Andrew felt that he could now pluck up the courage to ask Anna out. Andrew's knees shook at the thought, but he was determined to do it.

Optimistic, Andrew burst into the café. As usual, there was the normal Saturday crowd. Anna was standing at the centre of a group of people Andrew didn't recognise, happily talking to them. They all appeared to be roughly around the same age and they seemed to be dancer types. There were three men and four girls. Andrew guessed that they must be her friends. What if one of them was her boyfriend? How could someone as beautiful as Anna not have a boyfriend? Pearl was amongst the group, laughing and showing off a large diamond rock on her ring finger. Anna happily put her arm around Pearl's shoulder and kept saying that she was so happy for her. Andrew didn't care; all he cared about was how much of an idiot he felt for thinking Anna would ever consider going out with him. Andrew turned and walked out of the café.

Sunday, 7:30 a.m.

Andrew didn't sleep well at all. It took him a long time to fall asleep in the first place and when he did, he woke up several times in the night. He didn't feel rested at all.

Andrew was embarrassed that he'd actually thought Anna would go out with him. Maybe he was too focussed on her; maybe he should be looking at other options. At work, there were two girls that were roughly his age. There was a girl in the secretarial pool who he recognised from Portobello Market. For some reason, she had the impression that you should have an offbeat style of dress when you went to the market. She would parade around Portobello in the most revealing, over-the-top clothes; in her mind, it helped her fit in with the area. However, at work, she was very conservative in her dress and professional in her attitude and behaviour. You would never believe in a million years that it was the same person that flashed her knickers on a Saturday in Portobello Market. Seeing the way she was at work gave Andrew food for thought, especially since she was always very pleasant towards him.

Then there was another girl in accounts. She was a lot more laid back and serious than the first girl, and kept to herself. Although not as attractive as the first girl, Andrew felt she could be the more stable girlfriend. Andrew thought he should go with the safe option, reasoning that as much as the first girl seemed nice, she might have some wild habits that he was not equipped to deal with. That lesson he had already learned from dating Kadisa.

Andrew wondered why he was thinking about women all the time when all he saw in front of the mirror was a slightly balding, overweight failure. He still needed to get his act together, work harder, and continue to build a life for himself. That was more important than thinking about women.

Concluding that he would never get to go out with Anna and that he should concentrate on work, Andrew was at a loss for what to do for the day. Should he punish himself by going to the café or just spend his Sunday organising himself for the week? Like a drug, Andrew tried to convince himself that it would do no harm to go to the café for an hour.

Armed with his newspaper and notebook, Andrew walked into the café.

Andrew sat in his usual seat and right away, Anna approached him.

"Egg and Bacon?" she asked.

"Yes please," replied Andrew, smiling despite himself.

He watched as she whisked away to take the orders of another customer. Andrew saw the professor as he left his seat and walked outside for a smoke. He had to admit that he still found the professor's habit of constantly pacing around the café annoying; why couldn't he simply sit still? Andrew watched as Anna stood by the counter, took a napkin and wrote something on it. Alfie then gave her the egg and bacon dish, which she carefully placed on a tray along with the cup of coffee. She placed the napkin on the tray as well. When she put the tray in front of Andrew, he noticed her full name was written on the napkin, along with an address in the Czech Republic. He realised that for some reason, he had never asked her where she was from.

He made a point of thinking he would ask her about her country.

"What's this?" asked Andrew.

"I'm leaving."

You've got a new job?" asked Andrew.

"No, I'm leaving London, England."

"What?"

"I've had enough. All I ever wanted to do was dance, but it's too much. I am tired all the time. The classes are great, but London is too expensive and too draining. I'm constantly struggling to make ends meet. If I don't do something now, I will make myself ill with stress. Perhaps it is possible to have a nice life in London, but to do that, you need to make a lot more money than I will ever make."

"I don't know what to say," Andrew replied truthfully.

"It's okay, I've accepted my decision. I hate it, I hate the idea that I've given up on my dream, but this is not a healthy way to live. Anyway, you haven't shown me your art yet—why not send me a picture?

Just as Andrew was about to say something, a customer called Anna over.

Andrew tried to eat his breakfast but found that he had no appetite. Perhaps he should have asked her out earlier, but he simply hadn't had the money. Would she have been the type of woman that would have gone out with him anyway? He would never know the answer to that question now, as his lack of courage prevented him from trying anything. He was a total wimp and now Anna was going out of his life forever. Watching her serve customers, Andrew felt tears filling his eyes. There was a football game later on and people were already beginning to pile into the café.

Andrew felt an ache in his gut. He wondered if when she was gone, his feelings would go away. Perhaps it would be out of sight, out of mind; an obsession that needed her to leave for him to move on.

Andrew was so concerned with his fight to survive, it never really occurred to him that life could be better. The constant reality of just keeping his head down was all-consuming. Anna had been the one spark of hope that symbolised the possibility of life being better, he hadn't tried to grab it. He had never felt that hope could be enough, that it could lead to reality. In the past, Andrew had purchased lots of books on visualisation, but dismissed all of them as living in cloud cuckoo. He only dealt with the practical and wishing for something did not automatically make things better.

The fact remained that the girl of his dreams didn't see any way of *her* dreams becoming a reality. It was a feeling he understood, as it was the very reason he had been too scared to ask her out. It was also the reason he stopped creating. He understood that constant struggle, the feeling that your small wins were never enough. There were other people with high paying jobs that went on holidays, with parents who could bail them out when they were in trouble. Andrew had never had that.

Andrew thought of his friend James who, despite having all those privileges, had still ended up homeless. He wondered what it was within himself that prevented him from becoming homeless. The one constant that Andrew had was the feeling that he had to fight; it was the only choice he had to survive. He couldn't let his mother down.

Anna would go home to her family, take the time to figure things out. Would she respect the choice that she had made or would she accept that she had simply overreached herself? Andrew had given up on his dream to be an artist and yet now, someone was happy to pay five-hundred pounds for his work. It was that feeling of being valued for his skills that made Andrew feel that perhaps he was worthy of Anna. Something he had simply done as a joke was taken seriously enough for someone to buy it. That made him think that maybe, just maybe, there was always a small hint of hope.

Cliff, who had been chatting with Alfie, suddenly took a gift-wrapped box from under the counter and tapped a knife on a glass.

"Good Morning, Ladies and Gentlemen. I would like to have your attention please. I would like to make an announcement. It is with great regret that I must be the bearer of sad news."

"What! Are you leaving the country?" heckled a customer, to much laughter.

Adopting an air of importance, Cliff ignored the remark.

"Sadly, I have to announce that our wonderful waitress Anna will be leaving us to pursue pastures new."

There was an audible gasp in the café.

"I am sure that you will echo my comments that Anna was an absolute joy to have here."

"Anything or anyone would be better than what we had before," quipped another customer to the sound of laughter, "but we get what you mean."

Grabbing Anna next to him, Cliff presented the gift to her.

"Anna, you have been totally sensational and we have appreciated all your hard work. On behalf of Alfie and all the customers, we would like to present you with a small token of our love and appreciation."

"Thank you!" exclaimed Anna with tears in her eyes. There was loud applause.

"Now," Cliff picked up his guitar, "a song dedicated to you."

Cliff started to sing *Island in the Sun* and to everyone's surprise, he did have a wonderful voice. Anna stood mesmerized by his talent.

Andrew stared at Anna as her tears flowed freely, she was so incredibly beautiful. Bea entered the restaurant fully made-up and looking very glamorous in a new dress. She interrupted Andrew's thoughts by asking if it was okay for her to sit on his table. Andrew smiled and said it was fine as he was leaving anyway. He left the exact amount of money on the table and walked out of the café without having touched his breakfast.

Sunday, 9 a.m.

Andrew didn't know what to do; he couldn't face going back to the flat, so he started to walk. London was a lonely place for Andrew even though he was born there. He tried to imagine what it would be like for someone like Anna, learning the language, trying to study, making friends, taking rubbish jobs. She had made the café a special place for everyone there and yet she needed something too.

Andrew remembered his *An Officer and a Gentleman* fantasy; a fantasy that he would rescue the girl of his dreams in the same way. He imagined himself walking into the café, sweeping Anna into his arms and whisking her away. But the reality was, he simply had nothing to offer her.

Andrew walked into Tavistock Square and sat in the park, mindlessly watching the children playing. He buttoned his jacket to guard against the swirling wind.

An elderly lady was pushing a toddler on the swings and the higher the swing went, the louder the toddler would yell in delight, bringing a smile to the lady's face. Two children were playing with their scooters and a few teenage boys were playing basketball.

Andrew started to take an interest in the game as one of the boys, obviously the most talented among the group, was demonstrating the full array of his skills. He would dribble, feign, jump and score with such ease that the other boys could only stare in admiration. Andrew became so engrossed in the game that a light tap on his shoulder startled him. He turned around to see it was Lauren; she noticed his frown right away.

"I'm sorry I frightened you. I was heading to the shops and I thought it was you."

"That's okay, I was a bit wrapped up in my thoughts. What are you getting?"

"I'm going to buy some milk," Lauren replied.

"You're out of the way, aren't you? There are lots of shops nearer to our place."

"Yeah, but I like to take a walk around, it keeps me out of the house longer."

"Oh."

"I can tell you're sad," she said.

"Really?"

"Yeah, I can read your moods and most of the time when I see you, you are sad."

Lauren had that penetrating glare that Andrew always found disturbing.

"You're a mind reader, uh?"

"No, I just get you. Why are you always sad?"

"Life can be tough sometimes," admitted Andrew.

"You don't say."

"It's a lesson you will get to learn when you're older."

"I don't have to wait until I'm older; life is tough for me now. The last time I saw my real dad, I was four. Also, my mum is a horrible person."

Andrew had to admit that he agreed with her but found himself saying, "She is your mother, I'm sure she loves you."

"She hates me because I remind her of my dad, and she hates him."

Andrew was silent

"You look like my dad. He had the same sad look, even in all his photos."

Andrew was taken aback.

"Where is he now?"

"He's dead. Mum dumped him years ago and we didn't know where he went or what happened to him. Then we found out that he committed suicide three years ago." Lauren was in tears, "I'd better go, mum will be mad. Nice talking to you."

Andrew watched her walk away. He realised that her father must have died the same year he had moved into the flat. If he did look like Andrew, then her seeing Andrew around all the time must have been a bit strange. He sat in the park for a few more minutes before reluctantly walking off.

Sunday, 4 p.m.

Andrew woke up at 4 p.m., surprised that he had fallen into such a deep sleep. His conversation with Lauren stuck in his mind. All that time, she had seen her father in him, and he had always been so sad. Andrew wondered if her father suffered from depression; he couldn't imagine what kind of impact it could have on a young child to know that your father had committed suicide and worse, her mother could have caused it. He felt bad for Lauren.

Then he thought of Anna. He must be totally mad—she was leaving and he hadn't even said a proper goodbye. He didn't think it was his place to ask her to stay—after all, he hardly knew her. At the very least though, he should have told her how he felt about her. Did he love her? It was too soon, surely, but when was the right time to know if you loved someone? He had to talk to her; he knew now, whatever the consequence, he simply had to tell her how he felt.

Fuelled by a sense of urgency, Andrew put on his jacket and opened the door, surprised to see that Edward was just about to ring his bell.

"Andrew," he looked crestfallen. "Can we have a chat, young man?"

"I'm sorry, I'm in a bit of a rush. I will ring your bell when I get back, I promise."

Andrew rushed down the road. Edward was an irritating git at the best of times, and he definitely was not in a rush to speak to him any time soon.

The air was chilly, but Andrew couldn't be bothered to button his jacket. He simply had to see Anna.

The café was mainly full of men watching football. Alfie and Cliff stood by the counter sharing a bottle of wine, also watching the game. There was no sign of Anna.

Andrew rushed up to Alfie.

"Hi, where's Anna, is she on a break?"

"No," replied Alfie, looking at the screen, "she's gone, mate."

"What do you mean, she's gone?"

"I let her go early, so she could pack. She's flying out first thing."

"What!" exclaimed Andrew, thinking fast. "Okay, okay, tell me where she lives, I'll go there."

"Look mate, I can't do that."

"What!"

"You know how it is—data protection and all that bollocks. Besides, if she was really your friend, you would know where she lived."

"You are kidding me?"

"Sorry, I can't help you, mate."

There was a massive roar as one of the teams scored.

"Thanks for fuck all!" screamed Andrew, storming out of the café.

PART THREE

The Crush

The days went by with Andrew in a sombre mood. At work, he carried out his duties with his usual diligence but didn't have the energy or the will to join in any conversations. The girls sensed that something was wrong, but wisely decided not to probe. Andrew was grateful to them for that.

Andrew regretted leaving the café in the way he did. He might have felt better if he had at least said goodbye. He wondered if Anna would have been upset at the way he'd left, whether she would have been hurt, or whether she wouldn't have cared at all. What if he was just a reminder of the London, she no longer wanted to be a part of? Perhaps it was a good thing that Anna was gone, as at least he would now have a chance to focus totally on his life. Was he really in love or was it simply an obsession brought on by his loneliness? After all, he did have form when it came to obsessive behaviour.

When Andrew had been in university, rather than stay in Birmingham during the summer, he decided it would be a nice idea to come back down to London. James was going on holiday for the summer and Andrew thought that if he was going to do a summer job, he might as well find one in London and spend time with his mother. This was just before he started dating Kadisa. Andrew had found a job stacking shelves at Tesco on Portobello Road and had settled down to a life of home-cooked meals and trying to work as many hours as he could. He loved the idea of starting his day by having a coffee at *Kitchen and Pantry*, a well-known café with large sofas that he loved to lounge on. When the weather was warm, Andrew would sit outside, watching the world go by. Andrew loved the feeling and energy of Notting Hill and promised himself that when he'd graduated and had started to exhibit his work, he would buy a flat in the area. It just seemed to be the place he wanted to be.

It was then he saw her. She seemed to emerge from nowhere, moving with a slow provocative walk that allowed her hips to sway gently from side to side. There was something majestic about her as she confidently sauntered over to the bus stop, alert and yet in no apparent hurry. She was in her mid-thirties with jet black hair tied in a bun, with looks and a shapely figure similar to Sophia Loren. Andrew was smitten.

Andrew made a point of getting coffee at roughly the same time every day so that he could watch her as she went to work. Her style was roughly the same every day: a smart dress or skirt with a smart jacket. Occasionally, she would vary her outfit by wearing a jean suit or would send Andrew into the stratosphere of sexual fantasies by wearing tight leather trousers that showed off her figure.

Andrew figured that she must be from overseas, most likely Italian, as he found it very rare that well-dressed attractive English ladies travelled on the top floor of the bus; they tended to stay on the lower level. Andrew always felt people from overseas were fascinated by the uniqueness of the double-decker bus and found viewing London from a height added to the excitement of their experience. He imagined that she had probably been in London for about two years and spent most of her spare time exploring and enjoying London life. She might have studied international business and perhaps worked for a company that although based in her country, had offices around the world. In a few years, she might move to another country. Although she was always conservatively-dressed, something about her made him imagine that she would happily be found bathing topless on some beach in the South of France.

He figured that she probably didn't work very far away because she took the 23 bus rather than the 52 or the 452. The huge numbers that took those buses tended to go to Notting Hill Gate, where they could take the train to work. His theory was confirmed when, on a weekday off, he was wandering around the shops in Marble Arch and he suddenly saw her walking down the street with that slow sexy walk of hers. She popped into *Prêt a Mange* for lunch. Andrew stopped to discreetly watch her purchase a sandwich and his eyes followed her as she walked down Oxford Street and into *Selfridges*. He briefly considered following her into Selfridges to see where she went but decided that might be a little bit over the top.

He had spent the whole summer lusting after this woman and watching her go to work every day. It was the highlight of his day. He wondered if there were many guys out there that would alter their routine in such a way, just so that they could see their fantasy woman walk by every day. He also wondered what the woman would make of it; would it flatter or scare her? He did lust after Anna just like he had with that mystery woman and both of them seemed to be an unreachable sexual fantasy, but there was a difference. With the mystery woman, his imagination had never gone beyond the bedroom, whereas with Anna, he would fantasise about them dating, getting married and having children. Andrew wanted to have a life with Anna. This seemed impossible now though, as although he was in love, she was gone.

Lunchtime. Andrew was getting a sandwich from one of the many shops in the area when, as he was walking back to the office, he stopped suddenly as if he had seen a ghost. Walking towards him was a heavily pregnant Kadisa. She was wearing a very expensive suit and her hair was much longer than he remembered. She spotted Andrew and smiled.

Kadisa

"Hi Andrew, what's up?" she said, kissing him on the cheek.

"Nothing much," Andrew heard himself saying, noticing that there was an engagement ring on her finger.

"It's so good to see you, it's been a while."

"I guess it has," replied Andrew, shaking.

"What are you up to?"

"Nothing much, just trying to earn a living,"

"It's got to be done. What about your art?"

"Can't pay the rent with that," replied Andrew. "What about you?"

"I'm a Brand Marketing Manager for Andre Arnoult."

"Wow," exclaimed Andrew, remembering that he had read somewhere that Arnoult was an up-and-coming designer making great waves in the fashion industry.

"I know! It's an amazing job; brilliant perks and I get to travel a lot. Also, (excited pause) I'm getting married!"

"Congratulations," replied Andrew.

"Thanks so much. Well, it's so good to see you again." She grabbed Andrew in a massive bear hug and kissed him on the cheek. "I'm rushing off to meet my fiancé. We're interviewing potential childminders. Take care."

"Yep," replied Andrew, watching as Kadisa walked away.

Andrew slowly walked back into the building. He was still shaking and his entire body was cold.

He struggled to process exactly what had just happened. First, Anna was gone and now, out of the blue, he'd seen Kadisa, she was getting married and she was pregnant with another man's child. Andrew could feel his pulse beating at an incredible rate. He struggled to breathe, his head was pounding and everything around him was suddenly spinning. Andrew struggled for balance and the last thing he heard was someone in the background asking if he was okay. Then there was blackness.

When Andrew woke up, he found himself in a small room with a bed. He recognised the room from his first day at Kane Publishing, when Marcia had taken him on a tour of the building. He was in the staff sick room. Andrew staggered out of the bed and opened the door into another room, where the staff nurse was sitting at her desk, engrossed in her computer.

"You're awake," she said. Her smile was friendly.

"What happened?"

"You fainted," replied the nurse.

"Right, thanks for your help. I'd better get back to work."

"I don't think so," replied the nurse. "I think you'll be okay, but Jeff will be dropping you home as a precaution."

Jeff was the company chauffeur; a quiet, kind-hearted man who also doubled as the company handyman.

Andrew didn't have the will to argue. While driving home, Andrew still couldn't believe what had just happened. Why had she suddenly appeared now? Everything seemed to be working well for Kadisa; she'd obviously moved on but Andrew was

188

stuck in the same rut. Andrew realised that for Kadisa, the break-up was just a minor incident in her life; no more important than brushing her teeth in the morning. She didn't think or care that she'd destroyed Andrew's world. Andrew felt so inadequate around her. He wasn't being fair to himself. After all, at least he had steady work and he had sold a painting. Not only that, but someone wanted to see more of his work! Why hadn't he mentioned that?

Agnes called Andrew to check if he was okay. Andrew assured her that he was fine and that he would be back to work the next day—he knew that he needed to keep busy. As soon as he was home, Andrew slept until the morning.

For the rest of the week, Andrew followed the routine of going to work, going home to eat, and going straight to bed. One of the many catering companies he'd called got back in touch with him to offer four nights of bar work. Andrew took it, feeling that he just needed to be busy.

Having got home from work on the Friday evening, he saw Edward standing in front of his flat.

"I tried calling you last week. What happened?"

Andrew tried to stifle his annoyance at this man questioning him about things that were essentially none of his business. "I've had a lot going on."

"Never mind, I just needed someone to talk to. Charlotte's left me."

"You're joking," replied Andrew, genuinely stunned.

"Can I take you for a drink?"

Edward's Dilemma

The sound of Tom Jones' *Delilah* played in the background from an old-fashioned jukebox. A group of middle-aged punters sang happily to the music. They both sat in the pub in silence, Edward nursing a pint and Andrew taking occasional sips of his rum and coke, a tipple he had developed a taste for whilst working at the bar. Andrew couldn't believe that the broken man that sat in front of him was the same arrogant prick that he had known since he moved into the flat. Andrew didn't know what to do. He'd had a long day at work and all he wanted to do was go home and yet here he was, sitting in one of his least favourite places, fighting the urge to fall asleep.

During the early nineties, this was one of the many pubs that underwent massive refurbishments to attract the better-heeled clientele. The strategy initially worked, with the pub attracting the rich and socialite members of the Notting hill set. However, soon that clientele found trendier places and as their wont, moved on. The landlords realised that if they wanted to stay in business, they would have to adopt a different strategy; the prices were lowered, the décor was changed, and they were very grateful to the local community, who didn't hold it against them for trying to force them out over the last few years. Many of them returned to drink at the pub. Andrew was initially surprised that Edward had chosen this pub to meet in; it didn't seem his style somehow.

"So, how are you, young man?"

"I'm okay," replied Andrew.

"How's work?" asked Edward.

"Work's okay," replied Andrew, realising that this was the first time Edward had ever asked him about work. This was no surprise because as far as Edward was concerned, his favourite topic of conversation was always himself. Andrew covered his mouth to hide the fact he was yawning. This was getting tedious, and he realised that if he didn't bring things up and force the issue, they could be there all night. He wasn't sure he would be able to last the evening.

"I'm so sorry to hear about you and Charlotte, what happened?" he asked.

"She's been having an affair with Javier," Edward blurted out.

"You're joking!" exclaimed Andrew. He suddenly remembered the incident in Hyde Park, when Javier had touched Charlotte's bum. "My God!"

"It's true," replied Edward.

"I don't understand, you guys were made for each other," said Andrew.

"I thought so too, but it doesn't appear to be the case, does it, young man!" Edward suddenly shouted. Seeing Andrew's face flash with anger, Edward slumped into his chair. "I'm so sorry, that was uncalled for, it's just I don't know what to do. This is so upsetting. We were always so perfectly matched. I still can't believe it."

"I'm so sorry, mate."

"It all started when she met that bloody Kwame."

"Kwame?"

"Her spiritual 'guru'," Edward snarled sarcastically.

"Her what?" exclaimed Andrew.

"Her spiritual guru. She wanted to get in touch with her higher self, to reach contentment and enlightenment, to be one with the universe."

"Sounds like a lot of crap to me," replied Andrew.

"It was, but Charlotte fell for it hook, line and sinker. At first, she would go to his meditation sessions once a week, then it became three times a week. It didn't bother me in the beginning. I mean, we were always open to new things and Charlotte's been into things like meditation, yoga and the like since I've known her. But then, all of a sudden, nothing I did was ever good enough. She started to criticise small things at first, like the fact I like my shoes lined up together in a certain way, or that I take my vitamins in a particular order. It had never bothered her before."

Andrew wondered if Edward was borderline OCD.

Edward went on. "Then she started on my clothes. What's wrong with wearing hoodies? It's a cool thing to do, everyone does it! She even went on about my bloody aftershave and she was the one that bought it for me. Then she moved to larger issues like our sex life, even though we had a very active sex life."

The thought of his now fanatical hatred of the EastEnders theme tune came to mind. He also had that eerie sense of déjà vu; Ansell had also come to him when Shannon dumped him. He must have that sort of a face.

"She wanted to experiment more. At first, it was just having sex on different days. What's wrong with the days that we had before? Honestly, what's wrong with having a bit of a routine? I just like to know what's going on, that's all.

"I get it, a man likes to know where he stands," said Andrew, trying his best to be sincere but having to cover his mouth to stop himself laughing.

"That's exactly right, old boy," replied Edward. "So even though the change of routine threw me, I still went with it, because I loved her."

"Right," said Andrew. *That explained the Saturday session a few weeks ago,'* he thought.

"Then," continued Edward, "she wanted to be more daring. According to Kwame, sex was the purest form of spiritual enlightenment and shouldn't be restricted to just one person. In hindsight, I wouldn't have put it past her to have slept with this Kwame person."

Edward didn't spare any details about what happened next; Charlotte had wanted to add more spice to their sex life, so she had initiated a series of new sex games, which Edward had initially been happy to go along with. The more Edward went along with those games though, the more extreme her ideas became. They had tried swinging with other couples, and during some of the sessions, Kwame had even joined in with one of his many wives. Andrew listened opened-mouthed when Edward explained that Kwame didn't believe in conventional marriage and that in order to maintain his connection with the cosmos, he had to share his wisdom with as many women as possible. Kwame considered Charlotte to be a noble disciple and wondered if she had a similar calling. As such, he encouraged her sexual experimentations. It didn't escape Edward's notice that Charlotte was also one of Kwame's wealthier clients and had the finances to continuously donate to his organisation of 'Spiritual Upliftment'.

Encouraged by Kwame, Charlotte concluded that her spiritual partner was her personal trainer, Javier. After this realisation, she came upon the idea of having a threesome to test it out. Although extremely uncomfortable with the idea, he had gone along with it, reasoning that they had been together for years and had both gone through various phases, including the odd affair, so surely this one would end at some point too. However, it didn't. Javier was invited around more and more, with Edward taking part less and less. She then moved the personal trainer into the flat and they shared a bed while Edward was made to sleep on the sofa. The shock realisation that his relationship was over, combined with the fact that the personal trainer was a lot younger and fitter than him, made Edward feel it was foolish to try and stand up to him. So now he had to make sorting out his living arrangements a priority.

Andrew found the whole story so weird. He found it unbelievable that people could live this way, and that all of this had happened right under his nose and he hadn't even noticed.

Having exhausted the topic of his own situation, Edward suddenly mentioned that he'd never seen Andrew with anyone. Didn't he have someone he was interested in? Andrew, fortified by his third rum and coke, told Edward about his experience with Kadisa. Edward was very sympathetic, saying that he remembered having his heart broken when he was younger and how much it hurt. When Andrew asked him how old he'd been when he'd had his heart broken, Edward replied that he had been eleven years old. They both laughed when Edward mentioned that the object of his affection left him for the boy with the larger train set. He refused to ride a train for two years after that and to this day, he hated trains.

Andrew went on to tell him about Anna. Edward commented that he never went to the café but even around his social set, people were talking about this incredibly beautiful waitress that worked in the greasy spoon on Portobello Road. Andrew even admitted that Anna was the reason he had been jogging in the park and they both laughed uncontrollably when Andrew described himself crawling along the floor to avoid being seen by him and Charlotte. Edward was surprisingly sympathetic and as they both sat deep in thought, thinking about their unhappy love lives—Edward nursing his beer, Andrew now changing his drink to a glass of wine— the jukebox suddenly started playing Neil Diamond's *Love on the Rocks,* causing them both to cry with laughter.

Saturday, 8 a.m.

Andrew fixed his eyes on his clothes as they tossed around in the washing machine, ignoring the Jamaican man and the African man as they rowed about certain points in the Bible. The Jamaican man was waving his fingers fanatically in the face of the African man, who was holding up his Bible like some sort of shield. The Spanish man stood in between them, preventing them from coming to blows. The laundry attendant watched the scene, her eyes alight with pure joy.

It was a week last Friday since Andrew had met Edward for a drink. He was surprised that Edward had wanted to talk to him of all people. However, he had slowly realized that for all his bravado, Edward was like a lot of people he knew; he had an air of confidence that masked a deep sense of insecurity.

Andrew walked out of the laundrette, ignoring the escalating shouting that was taking place inside. He enjoyed the sunshine and smiled at the memory of his drinks with Edward; he had to admit that in the end, he had enjoyed himself. He found himself subconsciously heading towards the café but then he remembered that he'd decided he couldn't face going there anymore. Now that he had a little more money, he decided to make his way towards a specialty coffee shop, one of the many that seemed to be popping up in the Portobello area with alarming regularity. *Cressor Coffee* was an unusual name for a coffee shop. He reasoned that the owners had tried to make themselves different, even though they were the same as any other coffee shop in the area.

After sitting down comfortably with his newspaper, Andrew saw Ansell walking in with a young girl of around twenty and, to his surprise, Lauren.

"What's up Bro?" exclaimed Ansell. "I thought that was you. This is my daughter Maxine. Maxine, this is my brethren, Andrew."

Now that Andrew looked at Maxine, he noticed the resemblance, particularly around the eyes. They both said hello.

"And of course, you know the lovely Lauren."

"Hi Lauren."

She smiled shyly.

"How's things bro, I didn't expect you here?"

"Moving up in the world."

"That's the first time I've ever heard anyone refer to going to a fancy coffee shop as 'moving up in the world'."

"In my world it is."

"Okay, have you been to the café lately?"

"No," replied Andrew evenly.

"Well, apparently your girl's not there anymore, she's left."

"I know," replied Andrew, not even attempting to hide the sadness in his voice.

"You know?"

"She told me before she went."

"Oh," replied Ansell. "Well, they've replaced your girl…"

Andrew's heart skipped a beat.

"…with some Goth looking girl. Big tits, man, with nice child-bearing hips. Not to sound funny though, with all the tattoos she's got, I get the feeling she's scaring the customers away. Why the hell would someone do that to themselves?"

"Don't have a clue mate," replied Andrew.

"Me neither. Don't they realise that when they get old and their skin gets all leathery-looking, that those same tattoos will look disgusting? I used to say the same thing to Shannon about hers."

"Yeah, that's true, but surely she can't be scarier than Gladys?"

"Not yet, but she comes quite close," said Ansell, suddenly changing the topic. "Anyway, do you know where she went?"

"Packed up and left the country, she couldn't take London anymore."

"You're joking!" exclaimed Ansell. "Did you at least get the chance to take her out?"

Andrew's silence spoke volumes.

"I don't believe this."

"She gave me her address so I could send her some samples of my work. But that's it, she's gone."

"I can't believe you didn't have the bottle to talk to her, but at least you've got her address." Ansell shook his head, looking at his daughter. She had the look of someone that knew more than she was saying, could Ansell have been talking to her about him? "I don't know what good it will do now, but you can at least tell her how you feel," continued Ansell.

"You're joking, mate, aren't you?" replied Andrew. "What's the point of that?"

"Dad's right," said Maxine. "You need to do that for your own sake."

"What's with you two? This isn't some cheap eighties American movie with those dodgy happy endings, this is my life you're talking about."

"You've got to admit, you haven't exactly been pulling up strings in that department," replied Ansell.

"Thanks a lot," replied Andrew, embarrassed. "Stop holding back; let me know how you really feel!"

"I'm sorry bro, you know what I mean," Ansell replied sheepishly. "Look, give me the address, I'm sure between me and Maxine, we can put something together."

"No way am I letting you do anything," spoke Andrew. "Anyway, what are you guys up to now?"

"We're hanging out together, doing a bit of shopping and then the movies."

"Sounds nice," replied Andrew.

"Maxine, take Lauren and order what you want. I'll take a tea—milk and two sugars." He handed some money to his daughter, who walked up to the counter with Lauren.

Andrew watched them. "Don't tell me you're back with Shannon?

"Naw, man, but Lauren's always had my mobile number. She calls me from time to time to talk. She's a good kid and Shannon doesn't mind her hanging out with us."

"Yeah, she told me her father died."

"True, that's how it is sometimes. I think she just needs a father figure."

"That's good of you."

"That's me," said Ansell, in a fake American accent, "I'm a regular nice guy."

"More like a joke," quipped Andrew.

Yeah, anyway, did you hear about Edward?"

"What about him?" asked Andrew.

"Well, he broke up with his missus."

"Oh, I knew about that," replied Andrew.

"Really, how did you find out?"

"He took me for a drink to tell me."

"What, you went for a drink with Edward? I can't believe I'm hearing this, I thought you said he was an 'arrogant prick'."

"He is, but I did feel sorry for the idiot."

"Right," Ansell shook his head. "So, you know about him and Shannon?"

"What about him and Shannon?"

"You don't know, do you?" Ansell had the look of someone glad to have some gossip to impart. "Well, hear the cry, as soon as Shannon found out about him and Charlotte, she tossed Yusuf's clothes out on to the street sharpish and offered Edward a place to stay. So now they are a couple."

"You've got to be kidding me!" replied Andrew, shocked. "Oh my God!"

"Yeah man, Edward is beating that one up now."

"Right." Andrew still thought that 'beating' wasn't a nice term for making love.

"Yeah, well, good luck to him. That's the one thing she was good at."

Andrew found it hard to believe that anyone would want to go near her. If he was ever desperate enough to sleep with her, he'd have to disinfect himself all over and get himself checked for every venereal disease known to man.

"I just can't believe it," said Andrew.

"Yeah, so it goes, man," said Ansell. Clearly, she was in the past for him. "Anyway, we're going to check out *The Black Panther* later, why don't you come?"

"Err, I'm not sure."

"Come on man, it should be good."

"Okay, I didn't even know that you were into superhero movies."

"Big time, man. I've watched them all. We saw *Wonder Woman* the other day. It was okay but I reckon Lynda Carter from back in the day was much better looking. She had some proper big tits too, man. I could imagine my head just vanishing in them suckers, man."

"Lynda Carter?"

"Yeah," Ansell got his wallet and pulled out a tattered signed picture of Lynda Carter in the *Wonder Woman* outfit. Andrew had to admit that she was pretty; he vaguely remembered her from one of those old 'True Romance' films, where the main character's wife suddenly announces that she's leaving him. Lynda Carter played the love interest.

"No way, you actually got a signed picture of her?" Andrew still stared at the picture.

"Of course, man. I was in love with her. Forget Farrah Fawcett, Lynda Carter was on another level."

Andrew didn't have the stomach to ask who Farrah Fawcett was, he made a promise to himself that he would Google her name at a later date.

"Look at that," Ansell gestured excitedly, fiddling with his phone, finding a picture of the current Wonder Woman.

Andrew looked at both pictures

"How can you compare that, to that?" asked Ansell.

Andrew laughed. Ansell could have a point. "You're a real piece of work, man."

"I'm right though," laughed Ansell. "Back in the day, I wanted to mash that Steve Trevor bloke up."

"You are so wrong." Andrew guessed that this Steve Trevor chap had been Wonder Woman's love interest.

"So, that's cool man. I'm taking the girls shopping and then I'll ding you around six, we'll make a night of it."

Sunday, 10 a.m.

Other than a thirty-something white couple engaged in conversation, Cressor Coffee was practically deserted. Andrew watched as a staff member went outside for a cigarette; he had long since concluded that it must be written in the job specification of every speciality coffee shop in the country that all staff members must be a smoker. They always seemed to be popping out for a cigarette.

Andrew imagined the café must be pretty busy by now. He could no longer face going there anymore though. He knew that at some point, the right thing for him to do would be to apologize to Alfie for being rude to him the other week, but he wasn't ready for that yet.

Andrew sat in the corner with his newspaper, a notebook and pen, and a cappuccino. He promised himself he would go back to bed afterwards. The night before, he hadn't got to sleep before 3 a.m.

The previous night had turned out to be a great evening. Everyone really enjoyed The Black Panther and there was an inspirational feeling as they left the cinema. Ansell couldn't stop talking about how good it was to see that many black people on the big screen, saying that he thought the film should be mandatory viewing for every black person, as it showed that when they put their minds to it, black people could do anything. Walking out of the cinema, they all spontaneously greeted other black people with the famous greeting shown in the film. This discussion carried on at dinner afterwards.

Andrew still found Ansell annoying at times, but he had to admit that he had such an infectious energy and a generous spirit. His daughter was another revelation to Andrew; a bright, intelligent girl who loved and was deeply protective of her father. Andrew could not imagine that Maxine had ever liked Shannon at all. In fact, every time Shannon's name was mentioned, she rolled her eyes.

Shannon's name was brought up because Ansell had asked her if it was okay for Lauren to stay with them during the week. Ansell had a huge house and was quite happy for her to use the spare room. Lauren found it hard to study at home due to all the drama and she didn't like Edward because Shannon insisted he used one of Lauren's cupboards to store his Viagra as well as his numerous vitamin pills. Shannon had said it was fine and that she could stay there forever as far as she was concerned. Lauren seemed happier than she'd been in a long time and Maxine was the perfect older sister.

Ansell, joined by his daughter, used the dinner afterwards to finally persuade Andrew to write to Anna. Despite the friendly ganging up on him, Andrew had to admit that he had really enjoyed himself.

Andrew looked at the letter he had written to Anna. It read:

Hi Anna,

I am so sorry I didn't have the chance to say goodbye to you. I hope that your journey was okay and that things are working out for you back at home.

I wanted to tell you something and it's something that I've wanted to say for a long time. I actually hate egg and bacon, the only reason I went to the café was to see you. You see, I really like you a lot. I think you are the most beautiful woman I have ever seen and I really wanted to ask you out. I think it's something I should have said before. You don't have to reply. I understand. Whatever, I wish you all the best in life.

Andrew

Andrew put his sketch of Anna with the letter and sealed the envelope.

For a moment, Andrew wondered if he should post the letter. He was scared. What was he doing? What if he scared her off, what if she thought he was stalking her? That bloody Ansell and his crazy ideas. Well, if the worst came to the worst, she'd ignore the letter. Besides, she was already gone from his life, there was nothing to lose. His normal routine seemed empty without being able to look forward to seeing her at the weekend. He had to post the letter, if only to provide some closure in his life.

In the weeks that followed, Andrew kept as busy as possible. On weekdays, he worked with Kane Publishing during the day and in a bar during the evening, having been offered five nights a week after doing a few evenings here and there.

At Kane, Andrew developed a reputation for being a very hard and conscientious worker and was given the additional duties of reception cover. Even though he was only a temp, he was also asked to be on a focus group that gave feedback on PR exercises. Andrew threw himself into the work.

After his day job, Andrew loved the change of pace of working in the bar. It wasn't a busy bar but the work was steady and Andrew enjoyed the fact that his co-workers were all actors and dancers; their excitement about their work and about making a difference rubbed off on him.

The weekends were filled with chores and from time-to-time, hanging out with Ansell, Maxine and Lauren. Maxine was proving a great influence on Lauren, helping her with her homework and general tasks, and Lauren had managed to twist Andrew's arm, convincing him to help her with her artwork. Lauren was surprisingly talented and Andrew enjoyed helping her.

Sundays would begin with Andrew having his normal coffee at Cressor Coffee before picking up his sketch pad and heading over to Ansell's place. After having some lunch, Lauren, Maxine and Andrew would go over to the park and paint. Andrew still had to come up with some new paintings for Jeff to exhibit. Ansell insisted all he had to do was to chuck some random colours on a canvas and it would be okay, but Andrew liked the idea of doing a big picture of the Houses of Parliament as a large lump of faeces. He decided to do both things, since the more he treated this as some kind of joke, the better.

From time to time, Ansell would ask if Anna had replied to his letter. Andrew would say no and that he didn't really expect her to either.

Javier

It was a Friday night just after midnight when Andrew strolled out of Ladbroke Grove train station. It had been a typically busy Friday night at the bar. He was relieved that his boss allowed him to leave early and told him not to worry about clearing up. Andrew stifled a yawn, grateful that the next day was Saturday.

At the taxi office near the station, and despite the hoodie covering his face, Andrew recognised Charlotte's personal trainer, Javier, carrying a suitcase. Javier spotted him, so Andrew waved.

Looking a bit agitated, he smiled at Andrew and said, "How are you?"

"I'm good," replied Andrew, eyeing the suitcase. "Going on holiday?"

"Not really, my friend," replied Javier. "I'm going to stay with some friends until I can get my shit together."

"Right," replied Andrew.

"That fucking old woman was driving me crazy. This was supposed to be some fun—fun, that's all. I just needed a place to stay. Every single minute of the day, she wanted to go here, go there and go everywhere as if we were a couple. We are not a fucking couple. If it wasn't the bridge club, it was salsa dance classes or even worse, art gallery openings. She doesn't understand there are women out there that would at least pay for me to go to these things. Why would I want to do that with her, for free? I'm a very busy man, why the hell would I want to spend precious time sitting in boring dinner parties or sailing? What the hell am I doing sailing? I hate boats. Doesn't she ever slow down? I have to earn a living and to do that, I need my rest. Then on top of everything, she wants jiggy-jiggy, morning, noon and night. And for some fucking reason, she gets even more turned on when that boring English soap opera EastEnders comes on. What's that all about? Who watches that junk? A bunch of ugly people who only travel from the chip shop to the pub—that is insane. I can't do my business. I'm losing clients because of her and I just can't keep going on like this."

Andrew struggled to hide his laughter. "Wow, man."

"I'm out man, out."

"I guess you've got to do, what you've got to do."

"Got to be done, see you later my friend."

Andrew watched as a man from the minicab office ushered Javier into a cab. Then he walked home, amused by this latest turn of events. He wondered if Edward knew about it and if he did, what he would make of it. He knew that Edward was still seeing Shannon because from time to time, Andrew would see him holding the hands of her children as she clicked and clacked down the street on those ridiculously high heels of hers.

Opening the door of the flat, Andrew spotted the usual array of bills. In the middle of that pile, was a letter addressed from the Czech Republic. Anna had replied.

The Letter

The phones were busier than usual and for the twenty minutes that Andrew covered reception, the calls were non-stop. Having worked in reception for a while, Andrew had perfected the art of getting callers to get to the point quickly, and he was grateful that he didn't have to announce calls.

Due to the increase in business, the powers-that-be felt there was now a need for a second receptionist to work during the busy hours. The idea was to have someone come in to cover from 10-2 p.m.; the pay wasn't that bad and the package was fairly generous. In keeping with the company policy, the job was geared to a parent with school-aged children or a retiree. The interview process had already begun, with Agnes providing the candidates. The person would be taken on initially on a six-month contract. Daniele, the current receptionist, was enjoying her new role as part of the interviewing team and during the interviews, Andrew was asked to cover the reception desk.

Andrew didn't mind that at all and found that by working reception, he got a more rounded idea of who worked where. In fact, he was surprised to find that after doing it for a while, he knew more about who worked in the company than Donna and Andi. The company was known for its many social events throughout the year. However, there were still people content to work in their respective departments without interacting with anyone else unless it was absolutely necessary.

After an hour, Danielle returned. Andrew had gotten to know her very well since working there and he liked her. She was a very bouncy character with a love of cheesy pop songs.

"Wow, that was brilliant; we've whittled down the candidates to two people. I've got another meeting at three, can you cover?"

Andrew had quite a bit of work on but replied, "That shouldn't be a problem. See you later."

Taking the internal phone next to Danielle, Andrew dialled a number; Donna's voice answered the phone.

"Hi, Danielle."

"Actually, it's me, Andrew."

"Oh, finished skiving?"

"Yep," laughed Andrew. "I'm taking some deliveries down to the mailroom and I'll see you in a bit."

"Hurry up, I could murder a cup of tea."

"Okay."

Andrew put the phone down and collected a box from the side of the reception desk, then he headed towards the mailroom.

The mailroom was buzzing with activity and the guys were stamping away. The director of the accounts department was helping to load boxes; he often visited the mailroom under the pretence of coming to give them a hand but in reality, it was his excuse to talk football with the group. Andrew dropped the boxes into the right area, with Peter thanking him.

"If you're in a bind, I can give you a hand if you like?"

"That's nice of you mate, we're okay for now."

Andrew walked back to the office, where Donna and Andi were busy working and chatting. Taking the cups, Andrew walked towards the tearoom.

It had been a few days since Andrew had received the letter from Anna and he was still too afraid to open it. When hanging out with Ansell and the girls on Sunday, Andrew had decided not to tell them about Anna's letter, as he couldn't cope with their reaction. It was far better for them to think that Anna hadn't answered back. They spoke about Charlotte's reaction to being deserted by Javier. Andrew had recently seen her walking down the street dressed in her dressing gown with smudged make-up, which was obviously not her usual standard of dress. Andrew was ashamed of himself; normally he would have walked past her but he had found himself being a bit nosey and asking if she was okay. She mumbled that she was an old lady that had made a great big mess of her life. She now realised that Edward was perfect for her, and she didn't know what she was going to do. In telling the story to Ansell, he said it felt very strange having Edward living with Shannon, and Charlotte now on her own.

Taking the tea back to the girls, Andrew sat at his desk. The letter was in his back pocket all the time. He thought it would be a good idea to read it now, in the company of others. If it was bad news, which he expected, at least in the company of the girls he would be forced to still have some measure of control. He nervously tore open the letter.

My dear Andrew,

I am so sorry to have taken such a long time to answer your letter. Things did not go as well for me here as I had hoped. I now realise that in life, sometimes you cannot go backwards. I love my family, but I now find that I cannot live with them anymore. So I have found a place to stay, I share with two other girls. It is temporary until I decide what my next move should be. I have a job; I am a manager in a restaurant. It's okay, but it's not dance. It pays my bills and I guess that will have to do for the moment. I am not happy, but I need a stable environment for a bit longer. Your letter was so sweet and when I read it, my heart soared. I always knew you didn't like egg and bacon—it's awful food, isn't it? I was willing you to ask me out because I felt the same as you. I often wonder if London would have been a better place if we had faced it together.

Please write soon, Anna. X
P.S. Your sketch was so sweet; it made me dance around my room.

Andrew put his head on the desk and sobbed.

The Call

It was a call that Andrew knew that he would have to make. He realised that there would never be a perfect time to make it. Ideally, he would love to make the call when he was a successful artist and owned a large house in Notting Hill. Andrew was not certain that this was ever going to happen though. He knew that his current situation wasn't perfect by a long shot. His job was only temporary and wasn't what he wanted to do, nor was it challenging, but he was earning money. He also had the £500 from selling that painting. As such, he was able to cover some of his bills. The bar job was lasting longer than he'd thought and he'd started painting again. Andrew wondered if he should at least be grateful that things were slowly looking up, but he didn't feel that way. There was this hole in his life and in his attitude that needed to be filled. It was now time to call his mother.

It was Ansell who had finally made him call his mother. It wasn't something that Ansell nagged him about—although he could be good at that too—but when Ansell's mother died, it caused Andrew to think.

It had been a normal Sunday and Andrew had been ringing the bell of Ansell's house. As soon as Maxine opened the door, Andrew sensed something was wrong. He could see that she had been crying and all she would say was that her grandmother had died. When Andrew had entered the house, Ansell was sitting at the kitchen table in tears, looking at a photo album. Lauren was sitting next to him.

Andrew hadn't known what to do, so he'd just sat there with them in silence.

Ansell wanted Andrew to come to the funeral with him, but he felt a bit uncomfortable about that because he wasn't family. However, he promised that he would come with him to the reception later. The family all gathered at Ansell's house, where a huge picture of Ansell's mother was prominently displayed in the centre of the room. The woman had a look of having dealt with hardship with the steely determination of someone that refused to let the world beat her down. Andrew did not realise that Ansell had such a big family, but he soon learned as they all gathered around to mourn. Ansell's elder daughter, Loretta, had flown in from the states to be with them. Andrew remembered Ansell telling him that she had graduated from Harvard University and had some top position in a bank.

Everyone had something to say and Andrew listened to speech after speech about Ansell's mother. The bulk of them talking about how, as a strong-willed woman, she had single-handily dragged the family, sometimes kicking and screaming, to all get an education and to always live a life of honesty and integrity. Ansell's speech was a particularly emotional one, as he told of how she influenced him as a man and said that even at his age, he still feared doing something out of turn in case he would get a clip round the ear. He brought tears of laughter when describing how, as a child, he was embarrassed at his mother's habit of standing in the market, casually eating the fruits on sale without paying, and then complaining to the trader about the bad quality of the produce he was selling. When he was older, he found out that everyone of Caribbean descent had a mother or grandmother with the same habit.

By the end of Ansell's emotional and humorous speech, there was not a dry eye in the house. Even Andrew found himself turning his face away to hide the fact he was crying, only for Lauren to catch him and by way of comfort, hold his hand.

At the end of the speech, they played Ansell's mother's favourite music: *Wide Awake in a Dream.* Despite the northern soul feel of the song, the tune seemed familiar to Andrew and it was only when they played the Barry Biggs reggae cover of it, that he realised he recognised the song from his mother's old collection. Andrew made a note to buy the original version. They then played Delroy Wilson's *Better Must Come,* another favourite of Ansell's mother. Like everyone in the room, Andrew found himself singing and dancing along with careless abandonment.

Andrew's hand trembled as he dialled the number and immediately, the familiar Jamaican accent spoke.

"Hello?"

"Hello, mum."

"Andrew?"

"Yes, it's me."

"Andrew, oh my days, I prayed that one day you'd call. What a lovely surprise. How are you?"

"I'm okay."

"You sure, why didn't you call before?"

"It's a long story."

Right then, Andrew let it all out. He spoke with a vulnerability that he'd not had with his mother for a long time, and all she did was listen. When he was done, she told him that as a son, he was everything she had ever wanted in a man and that she was so proud of him. That he must never be afraid to reach out to her, that she was his mother, and that she would always be there for him.

Andrew's mother described her life with his aunt. They managed to build their dream house and were making some major inroads in the property business—not bad after spending most of her life looking after other people's kids and cleaning houses.

She said that she wanted him to come to see her in Florida and that she would book a flight for him in the summer, so that he could have a holiday with her. When Andrew put the phone down, he felt lighter than he had in years.

Saturday, 8 a.m.

It was a typical Saturday morning; Andrew had just finished putting his clothes in the washing machine and walked out of the laundrette. He immediately spotted Edward walking down the street, holding the hands of Shannon's two sons. Shannon was confidently strutting two yards ahead of him. Andrew waved at Edward, who managed a brief smile before returning to a frown. Edward looked so miserable; Andrew felt there was nothing that he could do about that.

At least he felt a little better because he had finally taken some action regarding his friend, James. It wasn't much but he hoped that it would be the start of a better life for him. It was Andrew's conversation with his mother that had finally spurred him into action. In sharing his recent experiences with his mother, Andrew told her what had happened to James and her first reaction was to ask if his parents knew. Andrew replied that he didn't know, he only got the impression that James had fallen out with them. His mother said that he had to do the right thing and let them know. Andrew reluctantly agreed, despite fearing that they would resent him interfering. The phone call was tense, mainly because not only had they not known he was homeless, but they also felt embarrassed that it had taken Andrew to tell them. However, the conversation ended on a good note, with James' parents promising they would try to find him and do everything in their power to help him. They even offered to invite him over to dinner by way of thanks. Andrew politely declined, reasoning that for the moment, James must be their only priority and they were about to face some challenging times ahead.

Andrew's mind went on to Bea (who like James, lived on the streets). Since Anna had left, she seemed to have regressed to a state even worse than before. Days ago, he spotted her walking the streets, carrying all her shopping bags and mumbling to herself. Her hair was uncombed and she smelt of a combination of urine and faeces. The rejuvenating effect Anna had caused was gone forever.

On his way to *Cressor Coffee*, Andrew suddenly decided to stroll up to the site where the café used to be. It had been two months since Anna left, and he'd never returned to the café, but now he had to see for himself that it was truly gone. It was, and in its place was a pop-up store. Andrew just stood there, staring at the store. Two shopkeepers were enthusiastically hanging up the usual tourist paraphernalia. There was loud dance music blaring in the store and inside, Andrew could see rows of t-shirts, hats, key rings, and so on, with either the words *'Notting Hill'*, *'Portobello Road'* or *'London'* written on them. For variety, there were also t-shirts with English football teams on display. There were already numerous similar shops along Portobello Road; Andrew wondered how they could possibly make any money with all that competition around them. The excitement the salespeople seemed to have whilst going about their work was something he'd seen time and time again; in a matter of two years (as with *Cressor Coffee*), he expected to see the bailiff sign outside the shop and the business would be yet another victim of high rents and uninterested customers. It was like the cycle of life, with the excitement of a birth, a new life entering the world; only for years later, the sadness of death as that same life left.

Andrew was wondering how come he had such morbid thoughts when he felt this strange chill run throughout his body. He was surprised to see the professor standing next to him and it was quite apparent that he had been there for a while. Andrew smiled nervously at him. The professor stared at him before looking at the site where the café used to be. They both just stood there. The professor suddenly turned to Andrew and nodded; Andrew nodded back and watched as the professor walked away. Andrew watched the professor's slow, lumbering walk up the Portobello Road until he was out of sight. There was something about the way the professor was that made Andrew sense that he was never going to see him again. It was the end of an era, and Andrew felt a bit sad at that.

According to Ansell, the bailiffs had taken possession of the site, which confused Andrew, who had assumed that despite the low prices, Alfie must have been making money. But apparently Alfie had been struggling for a while, and with the rent being put up, it was only a matter of time before his business would shut down. It seemed that Anna's appearance had temporarily lifted his fortunes and afforded him a stay of execution. Also, unbeknown to Alfie, Gladys had been systematically taking money out of the tills for years. After a succession of waitresses tried working in the café at the weekends before going to pastures new, Gladys spent the last few weekends working there.

In the meantime, rumour had it that Gladys had emigrated to Spain to chill out in her Spanish flat and was using her additional funds to pay for the services of Spanish toy boys that would attend to her every sexual need.

Later, Andrew sat in the coffee shop reading his newspaper and enjoying his coffee. He took out his notebook, then remembered that his phone bill was due and since he had yet to set up an online account, he was going to have to pay it at the post office. The TV licence collection agency had also sent another threatening letter; Andrew had been ignoring it, reasoning that since he didn't have a TV, there was no point in paying for a TV licence. Now he decided that perhaps he should pay for it, since sooner or later he would get a TV, even though it wasn't the most pressing thing for him to do. Once those bills were paid, Andrew had to take into consideration that his rent would be due soon and since he had set up a standing order for that, he wanted to keep checking that he had enough in the bank to cover it. The evening bar job would be lasting another week; he would start calling agencies to see if he could pick up some more evening work. He also needed to call Jeff later that day to see if any of his paintings had sold; Jeff loved them both but confessed that he preferred the one with all the colours. When Ansell heard that, he suggested that for his next work, everyone should just toss paint on the canvas with their backs facing the other direction. They could be millionaires by next year.

Andrew checked the time; it was 9:05 a.m. and the post office would be open now. He checked that the letter he'd written to Anna was still inserted in his notebook.

Walking out of Cressor Coffee, Andrew saw Ansell, who was carrying a load of groceries and was having a lively conversation with Cliff. With him was Maxine, Lauren and Loretta, who had decided that after the funeral she wanted to spend a little more time with her father before she returned to the states. Apparently, Shannon never asked about Lauren, who was very happy living with Ansell and Maxine. Andrew wondered what the authorities thought about that. Ansell had mentioned that Charlotte had contacted him to chat and they had gone on a date. He wasn't sure where it was going, but he had said lustfully that she was "proper fit".

Ansell smiled when he spotted Andrew.

"What's up, bro?"

"Nothing much," replied Andrew, acknowledging everyone. Cliff gave him a big smile. "Just the usual, I've got my clothes in the laundrette and I'm heading to the post office. Cliff, what are you doing hanging with these lowlifes?"

"You're right, you know, my standards seem to have dropped dramatically."

They all laughed.

Andrew showed Ansell the letter. They bumped fists.

"Look, we're all going to have some breakfast after I drop this stuff off, you want to come?" invited Ansell.

"Sounds cool, I'll ding you after this."

"Ire, just remember, it's about time you buy a bloody washing machine."

Andrew walked away smiling. He had to admit he couldn't stand the people in the laundrette, but he was used to his routine and when you lived on your own, sometimes bad company was better than no company. But on the other hand, Andrew had to admit to himself that in the future, he would have to consider purchasing a washing machine. He would worry about that another day.

Andrew's mother had kept her promise and paid for him to fly out to Florida. It would be timed for when he finished his six-month assignment with Kane Publishing.

After leaving the post office, Andrew thought about the letter he had written to Anna.

Anna,

Thank you for your letter. I can't begin to describe how you made me feel. I have so many regrets and you and I not getting to know each other is one of them. A lot has happened to me, but more and more I realise that life is short and we just have one shot at it. I want to grab life with both hands. In your letter, you said that maybe London would have been much better if we had faced it together. So I'd like to ask you a difficult question: would you consider coming back? I know it's a big decision and, in many ways, I don't have a right to ask you, but I will. Anna, let's face London together."

Andrew posted the letter—for better or worse, it was done. Whatever the outcome, he would have no choice but to accept her decision. But for his part, Andrew knew that he had to learn to dream of better things. No matter how tough or difficult things may seem at the time, there had to be room for hope— there simply had to be.

Andrew dialled Ansell's number.

"Yowah," answered Ansell.

"I'm ready," replied Andrew.

"Cool, we can try out that new restaurant that Cliff's been talking about."

"Another one," joked Andrew, "I wonder how long that one will last."

Ansell laughed, "You got a point there."

"Yep, I figure I do. Anyway, I'll meet you there. I'm starving. I hope it's a proper old skool greasy spoon, I could murder some egg and bacon."

Acknowledgements

I would like to thank all the people over the years who have encouraged me to put my ideas on paper.

I would also like to express my gratitude to Leesa Wallace of Wallace Publishing, for all her hard work and patience in trying to make sense of my words.

I would also like to thank my wife and daughter, Nora and Natasa Thompson, for being my biggest supporters. I can't stress how lucky I feel to have you both in my life.

And finally, I want to thank my parents for the values that they have instilled in me that I try to live up to everyday.

About the Author

Lindale Thompson is a Latin dance teacher that lives and works in the Notting Hill area. Lindale dreams of owning a villa in the South of France and is currently working on his next novel, *"The Retail Park."*

Printed in Great Britain
by Amazon

47218091R00126